Chase
And Other Stories

Jean Bruce

ISBN: 978-1-7333748-2-8

DEDICATION

This and all other books are dedicated to my family, my friends, everyone who has ever believed in me, and you the reader. Love yourself and the world around you, for love's treasure is that it is versatile, infinite, and everywhere.

CONTENTS

ACKNOWLEDGMENTS

A special thank you to Quills for being amazing friends and an amazing audience, as well as their guidance and advice. Thank you to those that gave me the space I needed to write and to those that asked questions and were engaged with the stories who gave me the courage to continue. You are all amazing people and I am so lucky to know you.

PRINCETON'S JOURNAL: THE CRUISE SHIP

Rory, you wouldn't believe where I just was. I received a letter from the Sunshore Cruise line. At first, I thought it would be a discount or a scam, but when I took a glance at the letter the first sentence read, 'We need your help.' I was still skeptical, thinking it may still be a promotional piece of mail, but after reading further I realized this was addressed to me specifically. I don't normally get jobs through the mail, especially since I'm almost never home, so it struck me more than my usual phone call requests. For the past couple months most of my jobs were from overly paranoid types or small cases partnered with a string of bad luck and there was, of course, the Catacomb incident, so the idea of a relaxing cruise while getting paid for it was certainly appealing.

The Sunshore Cruise Company mentioned that there was a ship which had a reputation for being haunted. They used it to their advantage and offered tickets for the ghostly cruise which sold very well on colder holidays that were otherwise the slowest times of the year. However, they suspect something had gone wrong since the five ghosts of the cruise have actually been causing some problems among the customers. People were starting to get hurt. Someone had nearly drowned. They were asking for me to help them.

They offered me a handsome price and a free two-week long summer cruise. "This must really be hurting their business," I thought. I had other jobs that were waiting for my response, but I'd be lying if I didn't say that the idea of going on my first cruise, even with it so close to winter, was too tempting to ignore. I responded immediately and began packing for the trip.

I was let down when I got there. The disappointment came when I realized that I wasn't the only person they contacted to fix the problem. I was distraught to see the other person who answered the call. Jason Adams was there. I saw him and his camera crew doing what I could only imagine was an introduction for his show. I hurried into the cruise ship as discretely as I could, but he sniffed me out like a prison hound. "Princeton," I heard him cry. I started walking faster to the deck. The ticket taker stopped me and demanded identification. Jason was gaining, cutting everyone else in line, camera and microphone crew hot on his heels. I struggled to pull my license out to show the guy and nearly dropped my wallet into the ocean.

I got on the dock, but soon after I was cut off with a camera in my face.

"There he is, our own Princeton Figg," Jason explained to the camera. "World renowned Daemonologist, a career of his and his brother's own creation. Our very own elusive expert on demons, spirits and the supernatural."

"Jason get that camera out of my face," I demanded.

"He may not be a friendly fella, but he sure knows his stuff," Jason continued.

I ducked past the cameraman's arms and Jason's massive torso to hurry myself away, but of course Jason ran up to catch me. "Hey, Princeton," He grabbed my arm. I turned to face him.

"If you don't let go of my arm right now I'm going to kick your ass."

Jason let me go, knowing my threat was an empty one. He held his massive hands up in defense. "I get it Prince, I get it. I'm sorry about that time in the Espémort catacombs. I swear I had no idea the spirits there were that hostile."

"That's exactly your problem, Jason," I grumbled. "You have no idea."

"You do though," Jason replied. "And don't forget, it's 'Phaser' in front of the camera."

"Oh, I'm sorry, I didn't mean to damage your image," I spat. "But it doesn't matter. I'm not going to be on camera."

"Prince, buddy, why are you even doing taking a job like this? I thought you stayed away from high profile hauntings."

"Well," I tightened my grip on my bag. "I do usually, but…"

"Oh, I see," Jason raised his eyebrow. "They gave you an offer you couldn't refuse, huh? What was it? I'll double it for an interview."

"Get bent," I told him and made my way to the captain's quarters.

"If you don't, I'll taint your name as being a dirty hack!" He shouted.

"You'd do that anyway with the interview," I shouted back.

I was already regretting the job. I was sure I would get nothing done with Phaser McPhony compromising my work. I got to the captain's office. Captain Keisha Youngblood was written on a silver plate to the left of the door. I knocked on the door and waited. 'The nerve of Jason,' I was thinking. 'He always makes every job way more difficult than it had to be. I hated to admit he was right that I don't usually like taking work where it's crowded or highly advertised but damnit I didn't think he would be there. I felt called-out, but I just wanted to take a little break, was that so wrong? I still was nothing like Jason, always disrupting demons and spirits just to get a rise out of them for the camera. Him being there ruined everything.

"Well, come in," The captain called.

Her stern, authoritative voice snapped me out of my sour mood. "Right, okay," I replied as I swung open the door, my head reeling a little from the sudden change in emotion. Captain Youngblood sat at her desk, eyebrow raised, hands on some papers she was likely rifling through.

"Can I help you?" She asked.

"Um, actually," I fumbled for my wallet. "I came here to help you." I gave her my business card. She took it with a critical eye. She remained silent, so I took it as an opportunity to keep talking.

"I was given a letter saying that the spirits on this ship were getting more hostile? I called back a while ago and said I accepted the job. Did you... I mean, did anyone tell you..."

"I knew you were coming," The captain set down my business card and stood from her desk. "This ship is haunted by five spirits. They're a large selling point of this ship, a lot of stories get made about the ghosts here. You read the report, haven't you?"

"Um, report?" I asked.

Keisha took a small packet and tossed it on the desk. "The report. All the information you need is in there."

I took the documents and skimmed through them. There were a few photos. "A little girl haunts the hallway?"

"They're not always exactly at the spots you expect, but there are places each spirit seems to favor. The little girl is in the hallway of the bedrooms on the fourth deck, just above the casino."

"How many decks does this ship have?"

"Only six. Below that is the boiler room, where one of the ghosts frequent. Make sure to have your chaperone with you when you go down there."

"Chaperone?" I pressed.

"Mr. Figg, all the information is in the documents I gave you. Your room is on the fourth deck, room 402. If you'll excuse me, I have a ship to run."

I didn't have much choice. I could tell that the captain was either too busy to talk or she didn't want to have anything to do with me. I carried my bag and the documents with me to room 402. Other people taking the cruise were crowding the hallways, getting ready for their vacation. With the air being too chilly to take advantage of most of the perks a cruise ship has, I imagined the ship wasn't nearly as full as it could be. That just made me feel more claustrophobic. I opened the door to my room and, I have to admit, it was the coziest looking room I have seen in ages. It was like being in a deluxe suite at a nice hotel. A lot of the room was refurbished when the ship was turned into the cruise ship it was now. When reading the document, I learned that the ship itself was built in the late 1800s. Before, the ship belonged to a young aristocrat who committed suicide in his room now numbered 402.

"Aw of course," I darted my eyes around the room to see if I could find any ghosts, but of course I didn't see anything.

I read the bios of the five ghosts claimed to exist on the ship. The aristocrat in room 402 had the most extensive story. He planned a party on the ship the night all five people died. The young girl of the hallway was going to be his wife. Her parents and the aristocrat's advisors made the plans for their marriage. Even though the young girl was promised to the aristocrat, she had an older sister who had a reputation for philandering. She was keeping the company of the last two murdered men. The older sister was often seen on the floor deck or in the ballroom. One of her suitors haunted the boiler room and the last gentleman haunted the kitchen and dining hall.

In the documents was a photocopy of the aristocrat's suicide letter. In it he confessed to the murder of the older sister Nicole and her two courters, Adrian and Christopher. He gave the rest of his fortune to his wife-to-be, Nadine.

"Hm," I thought out loud. "Then what happened to Nadine?" I flipped through the rest of the pages but found only stories about their sightings and more history about the ship. I didn't bother reading anything that wasn't about the spirits themselves. I maybe still felt guilty for taking the job for the cruise. I struggled to read the final words of the photocopied letter. 'Sincerely, Lucas Wildeport IV.' "That's an oddly formal way to sign a suicide letter," I mumbled. I had a gut feeling, brother, that there was more to the mystery than what the documents read.

There was a knock on my door. After looking through the peephole, I wearily opened it. "What do you want, Jason."

"Listen Prince, real talk. We should work together on this case." My face soured. "Why?"

"I have a team of detectives that can help solve the murders of the five ghosts. I can get you any information you need. In return I just need you to help me get real, actual footage of the ghosts. You're like a spirit magnet and if you could just help me record them then we'll all benefit."

"Jason, I told you before. These aren't just mysterious beings you can exploit. These were real people who actually died and are actually suffering. I'm not going to help you make a spectacle of these tortured spirits just to help your ratings."

Jason pushed himself through the door and paced around. "Well isn't this one of the haunted rooms? Aren't you lucky? I wonder why you got this room in the first place."

"Get out of my room," I warned.

Jason turned to look at me. "This suite was supposed to be my room, you know. I had them switch our rooms because I knew you had the better change at having the aristocrat reveal himself. I would think you'd be grateful."

"I'm not," I explained. "Stop touching everything and get out of here."

"Fine," He raised his hands up in defense again. "But you'll come around. This mystery is too big for just one person. Speaking of which, where's your daughter?"

I felt a chill run up my spine. "None of your business," I growled. "Are you threatening me?"

"Hey, not at all. I wouldn't dream of hurting anyone," Jason started to back out of the room. "I find it interesting, however, how furious a parent can get just by the mention of their daughter."

"Whatever bye," I slammed the door in his face and bolted the door locked. I tossed the documents on the desk and sat there. I rubbed my face with my hands and groaned.

I watched the cruise set sail from the window of my room. I didn't want to risk running into Jason while he was going camera happy for his show. I tried to get some rest so that I could wander around the ship at night when it was quiet.

I woke up from my nap as dawn approached. The vision of the room was breathtaking, crimson and marigold hues brushed over every inch of the room. I was working on a new position to sleep a little longer, but I froze.

Someone was standing at the foot of my bed. It took a few seconds to notice that they were facing away from me. She wore a petticoat and held something in her left hand. In front of her, I could see elbows poking from her waist. It took a moment to understand that it was someone sitting on the desk she was looming over. I strained my eyes to see what she was holding in her hand. Slowly, I moved my hand to take my glasses from the desk. The vision quickly began to fade, I threw the glasses on, fixated on what the woman was holding.

The image was gone before I could see it. "Damn," I grumbled before my head hit the pillow again. I laid there, waiting to see if the image would emerge again. The woman in the petticoat, that couldn't be the aristocrat, could it? Who was sitting on the desk? What were they doing?

I got out of bed when I heard the hallway finally go silent. I prepared my EMF meter. I wasn't sure how helpful it was going to be at a job like this one but I figured it was better safe than sorry. While getting ready, I couldn't help but feel like I was being watched. I looked to the door. There was a peephole on the door but when I looked through, I didn't see anything. I opened the door.

"Oh!" I was surprised with the little girl turning and running from just outside. Before I could do anything, she disappeared. Three ghosts in less than an hour, it was almost too easy. I thought it could be a scam. Maybe the ship was doing some tricks to make the ship seem haunted and then hire me and Jason to hype up their sales. The idea disgusted me, but I had to follow my gut feeling. Something was wrong with the ship; I just didn't know what.

The ballroom was massive. It was in the same deck as the casino. I could still hear the night owls partying and gambling. The ballroom, however, was closed after dark. There was a locked door, but I was given a key to investigate if I needed to. I peeked to the other side of the door, first looking for Jason and his camera crew, then looking for the ghost. I slid inside and closed the door behind me. The click of the handle echoed throughout the empty space. "This place is ridiculous," I whispered.

I wasn't sure what I was expecting while I was in the ballroom. I stood in the middle of the room, silent, waiting. I could hear the dings and small chatter from the casino down the hall. I scanned the room, interested that they kept such a traditional feeling while also hiding LED lights near the wall of every room and hallway, as though the person who refurbished the ship made sure that none of the place would be immersed in complete darkness.

"Mr. Figg."

"Whoah!" I spun around and pushed away whoever was right behind me. I was mortified when I realized I just fiercely pushed away Captain Youngblood. "Oh no, I'm so sorry Captain, I didn't hear you come in, I didn't mean to push you I'm so sorry."

I offered a hand to help her up, which she accepted before standing back on her feet. "Well I guess I deserve it for not announcing myself."

"No, I'm in the wrong. I really should pay more attention to what I'm doing," I rambled on a few more apologies. Captain Youngblood snorted and started to laugh. I rubbed the back of my head and chuckled with her.

"You're definitely a strange person, Mr. Figg."

"Am I? We haven't really had a chance to talk much."

"Yeah, sorry about that," the Captain replied. "I get really one-track-minded during my shift and I had a lot to do."

"So, why are you here?" I asked. "I mean, it's kind of late. I would think you'd want to be in bed, sleeping."

"Well I was finishing up my work when I saw you in the security cameras wandering towards the ballroom. I thought I would have a moment to speak with you. I've been meaning to tell you and Phaser a few things that aren't in the document."

"Oh?" I asked. "Like what sort of things?"

"Just a few things that I thought I should tell you which is important to the case, but should be left completely discreet at least until after all this is over."

"Oh, well if it's discreet you're looking for, do you think it's a good idea to tell Jason- uh, 'Phaser' about it? There is one thing I know about the guy and that's that he doesn't do anything discreetly."

"Are you saying I should tell you and no one else?"

"I'm saying you should tell anyone except Jason 'Phaser' Adams."

"Okay then, I'll tell you and no one else," She winked. "The truth is, there is a sixth ghost."

"Who is she?" Princeton asked.

"How did you know it was a she?" Youngblood countered.

"I think I saw her already," Princeton explained. "Unless the one I saw was Nicole."

"Well, besides you then, I'm the only one who's seen this sixth ghost."

"Why haven't you told anyone?" I asked.

"Because I work for a company that uses every opportunity to make us profitable and I don't know about you but I want actual answers instead of vague bios. My great grandmother was Nicole's friend. She was here during the murders."

"What?" I was floored. "Is that another secret?"

"Yes," The captain replied. "I like my privacy. Still, I remember my grandma's stories from when I was a kid. I want to find answers for her."

I rubbed my arm. "Are you saying you want to help me out?"

"I have to work during the day and I'm too exhausted to stay up long at night. I can't do much to help, but I do have something that can be really helpful to you. Only problem is, it's an incredibly important heirloom for my family and I don't trust you to have it."

"Oh, um," I blinked. "Okay. Well what is it?"

"My great grandmother's diary. No one else can know it exists, do you hear me? Last thing I want is for it to be confiscated or something as evidence or some historical artifact. You're the only person I ever told it exists. I can't stress this enough, Mr. Figg. I need answers."

I nodded hesitantly. "Well, I'll try my best. But if I can't have the journal, how will I be able to see it?"

"Come to my office tomorrow after lunch hour. I'll let you stay and read it."

"Sure, alright. I will," I nodded. "Thank you."

I called it a night from there. I figured that I would learn more after reading the journal and the following night would be more fruitful. Before I left the ballroom, I had the strangest impulse. I thought about the boiler room and for the moments it took me to get back to my room I wanted to go down there so badly. However, I remembered Captain Youngblood telling me I needed a chaperone to go down there, so I clenched my fists and forced my curiosity to wait another day. I wasn't sure what the cause of the compulsion was, but I remember having gut feelings like that which were so strong it seemed almost like fate. I would have to follow it, but it would have to wait until tomorrow night.

There was a rapid knocking at my door. I did my best to ignore it, but unfortunately Jason never takes no for an answer. I got up reluctantly, stumbled to the door and opened it. I woke up instantly when I saw a camera in my face. I didn't have my glasses on, my hair was a mess and I was wearing my pajamas. I guess I should have known better. Jason doesn't know the word 'privacy.'

"Princeton, I knew you would deliver but I never thought just how much you would come through!" Once again, he shoved his way into my room. He set down a laptop on my desk.

"Jason, I swear to Almighty," I seethed.

"Remember Prince, it's Phaser when the camera's rolling."

"The only thing you're 'phasing' through is my patience," I told him.

"Prince be quiet and look at this footage," Jason demanded.

"What foot-," My eyes went wide when I saw it. I was in bed but sitting at the desk was a young man and an older woman looming over him. I hurried to get my glasses, face hot and red. "You put a hidden camera in my room?!"

"And good thing, too," Jason defended. "Look at this evidence. This is proof that Lucas didn't commit suicide. He was murdered."

"What?" I adjusted my glasses and took a closer look at the camera. I was able to see the gun in the woman's hand and it was pointing right at the aristocrat's head.

Jason closed the laptop. "Do you see now why it's so important for us to work together?"

"What I see is a lawsuit," I threatened. I started to look for where the camera was. "Where else have you been keeping cameras, huh?"

"I was given permission to put cameras in high-interest places for the case. It's not my fault this happened to be your room."

I turned to face him with my fist balled up so tight my fingers cramped. "Yes! Yes, it was! You told me yourself that you switched our rooms yesterday!"

"You could have requested a different room," Jason shrugged. "But why worry about that now? Prince, buddy, please let us work together. We can help each other out!"

"Last time we 'worked together' Jason, you unleashed a sleeping monster of the Espémort catacombs and nearly had me killed."

"Look, it was an accident. I'm big enough to admit that. Are you really going to hate me forever just because of one mistake?"

I clenched my teeth. A red vision of hatred grew from the corners of my eyes. "That wasn't one mistake, it was several mistakes. Mistakes you made by repeatedly ignoring me and every warning I was giving you!"

Jason put his hands up defensively. "Alright I get it. How many times do I have to apologize? I swear, on my own name, that if you let us work together, I'll let you call all the shots. I'll listen to every word you say."

I stared him down for a few seconds, but after a while I had to loosen my grip or my fingers were going to break. I sighed. "Will you get out of my room if I say I'll think about it?"

Jason grinned. "Good enough for me. But you really have to think about it. We both have something the other one needs. I can help you too, don't forget that."

"Fine, now go," I demanded. After I finally got them all out of my room, I fell face first into the bed. After having a couple moments to calm down, I went to look for the hidden camera again. I spotted it just under the window and pulled it off of the wall. I stuck it on the nightstand so it would stare at the ceiling. I wanted to break it, but I also didn't want to be responsible for a camera that was likely thousands of dollars.

After lunch, I went up to Captain Youngblood's office. "Captain?" I called in to the door that was slightly ajar.

"Just Keisha, and yes come in," She replied with the same focus she had the first time I met her. I hurried inside her room.

"Close the door."

I did as I was told.

"Sit down."

I did not argue.

She stood from her desk and pulled out the lowest drawer of a filing cabinet. After taking out a few piles of documents, she pulled out a burgundy-colored leather book. It was worn and pages were trying to fall out, but Keisha held it with the kind of care you'd see someone use for a newborn. I saw her hesitate to hand it to me. "Be very careful."

I nodded before taking the journal with both hands. I kept my focus on the journal even though I felt her stare on me like a hawk watching an intruder observe her nest. After a few moments, she went back to the work she had to do. I strained to read most of the entries. The handwriting was shaky and a lot of the words were misspelled. The ink was faded and pages worn over time. It took a lot of patience, but I started to unravel small pieces of the mystery. I learned about how Nicole's parents had all but disowned her. I learned how Nadine's betrothal to Lucas was ultimately their mother's doing. Adrian was the life of the party and head over heels for Nadine. Christopher was a kitchenhand, very gentlemanly and also head over heels for Nadine.

After a fight between Christopher and Adrian when Adrian pulled Nadine's petticoat up for the room full of people to see, that's when it happened. Adrian went missing. Christopher was poisoned. Nadine fell off the boat and drowned. Keisha's great grandmother couldn't believe the suicide letter either. Lucas, she claimed, was too sweet and shy to do something so horrible. Nicole, the 12-year-old girl, cut her arms and bled herself dry in her grief. 'I will never believe Lucas murdered my best friend and the boys. I will never believe little Nicole would take her life so gruesomely. She could never stand pain. Why would she choose such a slow way to go?'

I closed the journal and rubbed my eyes.

"Well?"

I jumped, remembering only after a moment that I was in Keisha's office. She laughed. "You sure are jumpy for someone who supposedly confronts spirits and demons on the daily."

"People are scarier, in my opinion," I admitted.

"Am I scary?" She asked.

"Well," I admitted. "You're... Driven. And, okay, just a little bit scary." I cleared my throat. "How much longer do you have to work?"

"My shift ended an hour ago," Keisha pointed to her window where the sea and the stars met. "Maybe you need a little bit of fresh air?"

"Maybe," I conceded. "Do you want to, I don't know, go out on the deck and maybe talk a little?"

She took the journal from my hands and put it back into its hiding place. "I think that might be okay."

"So," I asked as we walked in the chill of the night. "Is this whole mystery why you became a captain?"

"Not entirely," Keisha replied. "I've always been fascinated by boats and ships. I was really young when my great grandma died and I uncovered her journal as a teenager. I remembered how haunted she was at what happened on the ship, and I just wanted to give her some peace. It was actually through sheer dumb luck that I became captain of this very ship, but I wasn't about to let it go in vain. After the customer nearly drowned, apparently following Nicole, the co-captain was who suggested you. My bosses from Sunshore requested Phaser. And I don't know, I like his show."

"You like watching him fake and/or harass ghosts for ratings?" I asked.

"Is that what he's doing?" She responded.

"He has no respect for the dead," I explained. "He purposefully uses words and items and techniques to get a reaction out of them for the camera. He thinks of spirits and demons as props. He knows people are afraid of them and he feeds into that fear by making things worse."

"So then," She challenged. "What do you do?"

I sat on a bench. She sat next to me. "Well, I use science. I try to understand the entity to then find a way for them and humans to coexist." I explained my own journal to her. I mentioned it was really a collection of letters I write to you about my findings and my progress. I explained to her how you take these findings and record them into our books about Daemonology to help others try to understand these ethereal creatures we share the world with. At the mention of you, she perked up.

"You have an older brother?" She pressed.

"Not much older," I corrected. "But yes. We always say how I'm the 'doer' and he's the 'thinker.' Although I play a big part in the science and he's not without a few of his own adventures.

"So, he's the one that writes the books and makes sense of the science. That sounds really cool. What else does he do?"

So, we sat there and talked about you. I promise it wasn't anything bad, just how we both went to college and how you look after Sandra during the school days and some holidays. I told her about your gardening, your library and your silly tie collection. I also told her how much of a nerd you are. She seemed to dig it. Keisha is so much your type it's ridiculous. I gave her your phone number and I'm not sorry.

Soon enough, she was too tired to stay awake. I walked her to her room and bid her goodnight. It wasn't until I got to my room that I realized I never asked her about the chaperone to the boiler room. The impulse to go down and see it was even stronger. I wondered about going down to see if an engineer would be willing to just let me wander around for a bit. There was something I was compelled to see down there, but I was so tired from reading and my brain was so checked out that I convinced myself once more to wait for tomorrow.

I felt eyes on me in the dead of night. My tired brain fought me for the will to open my eyes. Everything was a blur and out of focus. I held my breath and waited for my vision to clear a little. Something was looking at me alright. A translucent man stood at my bedside. He was hugging himself, mouth downturned, face soured, tears rolling down his face. I wanted to call out to Lucas, but my throat was paralyzed in sleep. He saw me looking at him. He turned and walked towards the front door where he disappeared.

I struggled to snap myself out of sleep. Once I regained control of my arms, I rubbed my face to get rid of the tingling. It took a few moments, but I was sitting up and slipping shoes on my feet. Remembering the little girl, I slowly opened the door. She looked up at me in horror, her mouth hanging open in a silent scream. She turned to run, fading from view again. This time, I walked the same way she ran off to. I found the stairs to the main deck. I followed my gut, paying no attention to the time, letting the dim LED lights in every nook and cranny of the ship be my guide. As I got to the main deck, I saw an older woman run to the port of the ship. I chased after her. She turned, eyes glued to where I was standing, shaking her head and backing away until she lost her footing and fell off the ship into the ocean below.

I moved to look over the edge. As expected, there was nothing there. But as I turned around, I found myself face to face with another woman. Her scowl was fueled by hatred, and she motioned to push me. To my amazement, I felt a little bit of pressure on my chest. It nearly toppled me over the ship as well, but I managed to keep my footing. "That the heck?!" I cried before hurrying back to stable ground. I took a few moments to catch my breath.

"Did you get all that?" I heard a voice ask.

I gripped my chest and whipped around to see, who else, Jason. Before I had the chance to say anything, he put his arm around my shoulders. "So, are you done thinking about it?"

"I could kill you," I mumbled.

"Like how that mother ghost almost killed you?" Jason quipped. "With the right effects and music for that scene, man. Harrowing."

"How do you know the ghost was a mother?" I demanded.

"I told you, we can help each other Prince. I have detectives, and these detectives happened to find out that our murderer was none other than Nicole and Nadine's mother."

"What's your proof?"

"Well I already told you too much. If we're not going to work together then why should I tell you anything?"

He had me by the ropes. He finally had the upper hand. "Fine. We'll work together. But you have to do everything I say when dealing with the ghosts."

"Deal!" I shrugged Jason off but he gripped my hand with his stone grip and shook my arm like he wanted to play tug-of-war with it. "So, where to next, partner?"

I visibly shuddered. "First tell me how you know who the murderer is."

"I've already given you information," Jason challenged. "Now you have to follow through a bit before I reveal any more juicy details. Come on, where does that brilliant gut of yours tell you to go next?"

I was silent for a moment. "The kitchen," I replied.

"You want to get a midnight snack?" Jason asked.

"No, Christopher. That's where he was poisoned. It's possible that the spirits are reliving the way they died. This sixth ghost, the murderer, is who is causing the cruise to be more dangerous to people. If we can gather some clues, and possibly a motive, then we can find a way to either ward off the evil spirit or bring all of them to peace so they can all move on."

"I don't think Sunshore will be understanding about you exorcizing their main attraction."

"It's not exorcizing," I corrected. "If it's either resting the spirits to peace or adding to the death count, I think Sunshore can deal with it. Are you calling off our truce already?"

"No no no," Jason raised his hands up again. "Proceed. You're

14

the boss."

I hurried to the kitchen, passing only the occasional insomniacs and Phaser fans which his entourage had to keep at bay. They would give the fans pre-signed photographs and I couldn't roll my eyes any harder. We managed to make it to the kitchen without any real trouble but before entering the room I whispered, "Keep quiet. Don't follow me."

"Alright, Prince. We'll stay here."

I was honestly surprised, but I didn't respond. I unlocked and opened the door as quietly as possible. I wandered into the dining hall. I stood there in the dead silence, waiting. I felt a light, cold air as I sat at one of the tables. It woke me up a little and I looked around. Sitting to my right was Lucas, the aristocrat. He sat there, unresponsive. Forlorn. I looked to my left. Another young man was mouthing words, pantomiming to a plate that wasn't there, taking a bite. I felt a rise of fear. I suddenly wanted to scream, but kept my tongue. I watched as Christopher's eyes went wide. He put his hands over his throat, then to his chest. He sank to the ground, his eyes rolled into his head. Lucas and I sprung from our seats at the same time. I kept watching as Christopher struggled to breathe. Tears fell from his eyes. He fell face first into the ground. I turned to Lucas who spun and ran. 'The boiler room,' I thought. I couldn't hold it off any longer.

I ran out of the kitchen. "Jason, we have to," I stopped. A crowd of late-night cruisers were getting autographs. "Seriously," I asked.

Jason turned to me and grinned. "It's the price of fame, Prince." The people tried to talk and get Jason's attention. The camera crew were trying to talk to some of the guys and girls. "Jason cut it out. We have to get to the boiler room right away."

"Why the boiler room?" He asked.

"Just come on or I'm leaving without you," I turned to make my way to the boiler room. After some time, Jason shook off his fans and followed behind. I went as quickly as I could to the lowest level of the ship. I found myself halted by a large metal door. Through the window I could see a few men hard at work keeping everything intact. I banged on the door, gaining the attention of one of the workers. He hurried to open the barrier between us. He looked right behind me. "Is that Phaser Adams?"

"It sure is," Jason grinned. "We're here following a lead on some paranormal activity. Would you be our guide through the boiler room?"

"Does this mean I'm going to be on television?" The guy asked excitedly.

"It sure does," Jason confirmed.

The guy agreed to guide us through the boiler room to the place where the last ghost, Aiden, is often found. "It used to be the brig," The engineer explained. "You know, where you would put prisoners and stowaways. We're sure he died there somewhere but we're also pretty sure no one ever found the body. He just went missing and now his ghost haunts everyone down here. Hey Phaser, I just wanted to also let you know my wife and I love your show."

Jason laughed, "Well I appreciate that. You know, this redhead here is Princeton Figg, the very first Daemonologist. He's my special guest for this episode."

"Uh, no, I didn't agree to that," I said as I followed our guide.

"You did, when you agreed that we would work together. I have the proof taped. We shook hands."

Before I could protest, our guide stopped walking. "Well this is it," He said. "This is where we see Aiden the most."

"Thank you," I told him. I squeezed past everyone and started to scan the room. I closed my eyes, ignoring the steam and heat and the sound of Jason impressing the guide with his not-daring adventures and his not-accurate claims about the undead. I let my gut feeling take me. I silently offered for Aiden's spirit to take me where he needed me to go. I stood there for moments, meditating where I stood, hoping that something would happen. I waited, hoping someone would respond.

Soon I noticed that Jason, the guide and the camera crew fell silent. I dared not open my eyes. I didn't hear him speak. It was more like I felt what he wanted to say. 'Forward.' I took a few steps. 'Left.' I turned and cautiously kept walking.

"Prince," Jason called out. I opened my eyes and saw that I was face to face with the woman. She glared at me with empty eyes and thrust her hand forward as though to stab at me. I cried out in surprise and stumbled back. "Princeton!" I heard Jason cry and I felt his massive hand grip the collar of my shirt before violently pulling me back his way. I caught my footing, reflexively gripping Jason for support but letting him go once I was safe. "What's the big idea?!" I demanded.

"You nearly fell back into that furnace!" Jason cried in response. He pointed to the furnace I had walked in front of. "We saw the Aiden ghost take your body and you walked around that corner then nearly fell back into that furnace."

My eyes widened. "That's why there was no body." I looked up to Jason. "I get it now. I know what we have to do."

"What is it?" Jason asked.

"No, before I say anything for certain I have to talk to Keisha. Afterwards, you and I need to talk. No more secrets, I need to know everything you know."

"Fine by me. I got everything I wanted," Jason grinned.

Keisha had to work for most of the morning, but I was able to take her lunch break to talk to her. I told her how it was Nicole and Nadine's mother who caused the murders. I mentioned how I suspected their mother just wanted to kill the three boys but her daughters found out what she was doing. "Do you know if Nadine and Nicole's mother ended up with Lucas' money?"

Keisha blinked. "Yeah, actually. They were the Sunshores. Nadine and Nicole Sunshore. Their mother was the founder of the Cruise line."

I blinked. "I thought Sunshore was just a clever sunny name for the company."

Keisha shook her head. "No, Nancy and Edgar Sunshore were the founders of the cruise line, did you not read the history section of the document I gave you?"

"It was a big document," I mumbled. "I might have skimmed a little bit of the history section."

"Unbelievable," She muttered.

"Regardless," I interrupted. "Getting his money is motive to kill Lucas and if her daughters found out about the murders than it explains why they were killed, but I can't think of any motive to kill Aiden and Christopher."

Keisha shrugged. "When she was alive, Nancy Sunshore was said to be a violent and crazy woman. Maybe she was just being, well, violent and crazy."

I shook my head. "She waited for Aiden in the brig, right where the furnace was. She took the time to poison the food that Christopher ate. They were pre-meditated. She planned it. There had to be a reason."

"Why does it matter at this point?" Keisha asked.

"Because these spirits want peace. The reason they're re-living their deaths and the reason Nancy's spirit is still tormenting them is because this has all been a secret. Just like your great grandmother, these spirits never got closure. In order to fix anything, we have to expose the truth."

"How do you expect to do that?" She asked.

I slowly breathed in as much air as my lungs could carry before audibly letting it out. "I have one way in mind."

I didn't have to look for long to find Jason. He was in the center of a crowd in the casino signing autographs. I pushed my way through to him. "Hey Prince, here for an autograph?" He joked, or at least I hoped he was joking.

"Meet me in my room as soon as possible, I need to talk to you."

"So forward," He chuckled. "Alright, I'll be there in an hour."

Three hours later, there was a knock at my door. I opened it to let him in. "About time."

He walked in with his camera crew close behind. He sat on my bed, the camera crew surrounding him. "Hey, I'm here and that's the important thing."

"Okay Jason, I need to know what you know. How did you know that Nancy Sunshore was the killer?"

"I read the documents."

"Yeah but there's nothing in the documents that says she killed anyone."

"Come on Prince, get into her head. She was a terror when she was alive, a downright psychopath. I tried to clue you in from the start you know, when I asked you about your daughter."

"What the heck are you talking about?" I demanded.

"You got defensive when I talked about your daughter just like Mrs. Sunshore would have been. It's obvious that she killed Chris and Aiden for trying to get with her daughter Nicole."

"But Nicole was estranged from her parents," I argued.

"How do you know that?" Jason asked.

It occurred to me that it was knowledge I had from reading Keisha's journal. "No reason," I replied quickly. I knew I had to think of an excuse or look more suspicious. "Well, why would the younger daughter Nadine be wed before her older sister unless there was conflict there?" I countered.

18

"Regardless, a name is very important to most people. Especially a hundred years ago, a family name is a precious thing. If Nicole really was an easy woman like the documents said, don't you think a violent and likely controlling mother like Nancy would try to do whatever she could to keep Nicole from dragging the family name through the hot, sexy promiscuous mud?"

I took a moment to think about it. "You might be right," I mused. Why didn't I think of that? "So that's it, then. We have all the pieces."

"Sure, but what are we supposed to do about them?" Jason asked. "How do we, as you say, bring the souls to rest?"

My heart chilled at the thought of my next words. I didn't want to give Jason the satisfaction. "You have to tell the story," I explained to him.

"What's this?" Jason's annoying grin creeped even wider. "After being so resistant and giving me so much trouble to get the story, you want me to air it?"

A small groan escaped my throat while I swallowed the rest of it. "In this one, rare, bizarre case, I think exposing the truth is how we can bring the spirits to rest."

"So, you're giving me full permission to film all my footage to my show?"

My head felt heavy, but with great strength and clenched teeth, I nodded.

"And perhaps an interview?"

"Don't push it," I warned.

I signed the forms after reading them very carefully, making sure that Jason knew to expose the truth and to not fudge or alter any details to the case. Admittedly, I watched the episode when it came out. It was good, I guess. At least he took the case seriously in the show.

Keisha paid us both the rest of our commissions. I have a coupon now for a free two-week summer cruise. I've been thinking about it, and perhaps sometime in the near future, I'll go on a real vacation. I could come by Keisha's ship again to make sure things are going alright with the spirits after the episode aired. If she does call you, make sure you answer. If things go well between you two, maybe I'll mail you the cruise ticket instead.

JEIDOKYATTO

Deep in the forests of an old island, far from the clutches of humanity, where the beasts rested and the yokai played, an old woman took her careful steps among the foliage. She hummed to the spirits and breathed in the faint scent of burning Cherrywood from the fireplace of her wandering hut. Her hut followed her, floating undetected by anything that the old woman did not want as company. The old woman halted her wandering to bend down and gather some moss from an ancient bolder. Once she collected all she needed, she cackled gently. She slid the container into the sleeves of her weathered kimono and shuffled back to her magical hut.

"This should be plenty rock cap moss to finish this potion," The old woman said to no one as she took off her shoes at the porch of her wooden refuge. As she stepped through the barrier between outside and home, the old woman's shoulders relaxed. After a deep sigh, the woman picked up the clay jar of moss she put away moments before which waited for her on the counter of her home. She opened the jar and poured her prize into the cauldron at the center of her kitchen. The other contents of the cauldron responded with a bubble and hiss.

This old woman who lived alone was known as Baba, the witch of the dark wood. The living shared rumors of her and how she existed among the demons and spirits of this world and how only those truly in need or truly lost would find her.

Baba began to chant as she stirred her potion. The forest smoke began to hop and dance around the cauldron. "Take me to Jeidokyatto," She commanded it.

With a lurch and a tremble, the smoke wafted out of the door, snaking its way with purpose to its destination. "Eeeehehehehe," Baba cackled before shuffling back to her sandals and scooting her feet in the direction the smoke slithered to. She was led through marsh and meadow to the base of a mountain. The smoke floated before the mouth of a cave. The witch sat on a rotting trunk to rest her old legs. Moments after, she witnessed a sign of movement in the cave. Baba leaned forward and scrunched her tired eyes in time to see a glint just inside. With a huff and a heave, Baba pressed her tiny feet forward to greet the cave entrance.

She was careful to not rush in. She knew better than to threaten or fight. Instead, she bowed to the mountain's cave and reached into her sleeve. What she pulled out of her sleeve was a small porcelain cup filled with warm tea. Baba set it on a stone beside the cave before pulling an equal cup in her hands. She knelt before the cave and, eyes closed and hand steady, she began to drink her tea. The Trial of Patience had begun.

Baba would see the occasional glint from the cave, yet she did not move. The witch kept her focus on the sweet aroma of her herbal water, paying no mind to the slow, curious visit of the feline composed entirely of jade. The cat sniffed at the lonely cup before dipping its small, gem tongue into its essence. For moments, the timeless woman and the priceless creature kept the other's company with the silent pleasure of tea.

Once the cat had its fill, it turned its attention to the mysterious elder. Baba returned its gaze for the first time. She passed the Trial of Patience, but now The Trial of Sorrows would soon begin.

As their eyes met, Baba took note of the Jade cat's wise and mournful stare. Trinkets as powerful as this were rightfully an entity to fear, but that trial was yet to come. For the moment, the importance rested upon her unbreaking eye contact with the spirit. She could find the cat searching for the witch's saddest moments in her existence, only there wasn't much to find. Baba, unattractive and reclusive in her growing years, had no heartbreak and no regrets. The witch's mind dwelled on no catastrophe, no unforgiven weakness, no disappointment. However, she had arrived to take part in the trial of sorrows and in so there had to be sorrows to face.

The crying of the cat echoed in the air. The trial of sorrows would have to be done through the sorrows held by Jeidokyatto itself. The witch counted on this. Baba's stomach lurched and her body lost its weight as she felt herself floating in the air, the cat's eyes being her only focus. Before the witch was able to realize it, everything had gone dark.

Her vision improved to reveal a small hut not unlike her own. It felt cozy, but there was also a sense of dread. The witch's line of sight was much lower than usual. She felt emotions in a succession quicker than usual, the most prominent emotion being anxiety. The feeling became reality as she heard the shoji door slide open with a loud 'Bang!' The witch heard yelling but could not make out the words. This large man ran up to her and shook her violently. Baba had never felt so helpless. As he threw her against a corner of the building Baba never felt so trapped. Even as she was aware this was a vision; she could not slow the harsh rushing in her heart.

The next vision came suddenly. The transition was so jarring that Baba felt her neck ache. She was hiding in a cupboard, peeking through the crack at the man that shook her before. His presence felt like the end of her. She witnessed a young man enter the scene. The younger man cowered in the presence of the other man. He was a contrast, soft-spoken, slow and bruised. Scars and welts decorated his body. The younger man prepared a bowl of food on the floor and scooted it closer to Baba's hiding place. Around his neck there was a small, cat-shaped jade pendant.

A flash of lightning ignited the paper walls, rain poured inside the home from the slash in the shoji door. The larger man was shouting more and raised a whip over his head, his venomous glare keeping Baba paralyzed. The room reeked of nickel and mud. Slash after slash penetrated her small body, the painful wails drowned out by the storm, a limp hand resting just in view around the corner. Inside the hand there was a small jade pendant. As the last of Baba's consciousness faded, the eyes of the talisman seemed to glint with an inner light. Baba felt her essence leave the vessel she was in and take refuge in the small talisman as though she was retreating without being aware of it. Even as the world went dark again, Baba heard thunder and roaring harmonize into a woeful duet.

Baba opened her eyes. Inches from her face stood the trinket that grew to the size of a panther. Baba cautiously wiped the tears from her cheeks. The gaze of the being before her was her only focus. She watched as the creature turned and bounded its way back into the cave, shrinking back down to the size of a housecat. The old woman motioned to stand, pausing every so often to be sure she didn't harm herself by rushing. Baba followed the cat into the cave. As she left the sun behind, the witch pulled out a lantern and a handful of powder from her sleeve. She sprinkled the powder into the lantern, mumbling an incantation, and the lantern flickered into life. A dull blue flame woke the cave, veins of precious minerals catching the light. The witch paid no heed to the riches within the walls. She knew that surely if they were no illusion, they were a trial. In sharing sorrow with Jeidokyatto, Baba had passed the Trial of Sorrows and had to endure what she thought was the easiest judgement to face, the Trial of Avarice.

Baba recalled the things she was told by a wandering yokai. Jeidokyatto would only welcome those who were pure and calm. These trials were meant to test one's purity and kindness. Only when someone succeeds may they be granted the Jeidokyatto's protection. Baba thought about the visions given to her. The young man must have gotten the talisman to welcome serenity in his home, but the larger man had too much darkness in his heart. This spirit, the remaining essence of the beaten housecat and her unfortunate owner's final desperate desires, lived in the pain of the past for unknown centuries. Baba kept her eyes forward, aware that Jeidokyatto traveled just past the reach of the witch's dim light. As the veins of precious minerals thinned, Baba straightened her posture. She wandered further into the cave knowing that her final trial would be the true test of her worth.

The trial of patience was as simple as a silent cup of tea. The trial of sorrow revealed her empathy to the trinket. The trial of avarice would never be a concern to the witch who was certain she already had everything she would ever need. There was, however, one trial that Baba felt would not only prove difficult and convince Jeidokyatto of her worth, but if successful, it would prove her worth to herself. The Trial of Purpose was the last test.

At the end of the tunnel, there was a dull, pulsing light. Baba quieted her lantern and hid it within her sleeve. The witch was drawn to the slow beating of the mountain's heart. It beckoned her, whispered to her, needed her. Her pace quickened, the pulsing of the heart grew, it was just around the corner.

Baba halted. The endless tunnel was no more than a wall behind her. The old witch made it to the heart of the mountain. The pulsing of light was revealed to be torches carried by a group of angry men. The poor old witch stood cornered, witnessing these angry men as they pursued Jeidokyatto.

The men shouted and cheered as a net sprung from beneath the trinket, trapping it in its twisting rope. Baba froze in place, the sight of so many people left her frozen. She remembered the image of villagers with torches and weapons. She remembered watching the peaceful and playful spirits of the forest become lost at the result of mankind's greed, stubbornness and fear. She remembered witnessing the mistreatment of yokai and thinking that she had to do something.

The cry of Jeidokyatto returned her to the present. Baba reached into her sleeve and pulled out a hand-mirror. The witch looked into it, her reflection going black and her eyes glowing red. Her reflection opened its abysmal mouth, oil dripping from the reflection's maw. Baba turned it towards the mob and the oil-like substance bled out of the reflective surface. It poured out enough to create a large, red-eyed beast which was five times the size of any man. The oozing monster roared mightily, causing some men to run away immediately. All the others turned their attention to the large creature. To Baba's grief, the men advanced on the mirage, making their way towards the feeble witch. They continued to gain. Baba stood her ground. The only thing more terrifying to her than facing the mob alone was knowing that the mob would get what they needed from the poor yokai should she not intervene. The men were close enough to cause the witch to cower. Only a step away and, as though they were a memory of the mist, they faded away from sight.

Baba's beastly visage faded from sight. She was left there, searching for an answer in the cave. Jeidokyatto stood before her. Baba's arms and shoulders relaxed. The jade talisman and the witch looked each other in the eye. Jeidokyatto revealed Baba's deepest fear. It revealed the purpose of Baba's existence. When she saw the yokai in danger, Baba acted on impulse to do the thing she had sworn to do. Baba's soul was pure and calm, her sole purpose being to protect the yokai of the forest.

Jeidokyatto shrank before the witch's eyes until it was small enough to be clutched in the palm of her hand. It no longer moved or protested. It became a talisman of protection once more, and it was Baba's talisman to use.

The old witch cackled in triumph followed by a sigh of relief. She gingerly plucked the talisman from the cave floor and hid it away in the sleeve of her kimono. She turned to the reopened mouth of the cave and took her careful steps to freedom. As she reached the exit, Baba picked up the two empty cups from her tea-time and made her way to the safety of her floating home, now under the protection of Jeidokyatto.

WINDOWS

Ever since Arlene was a child, she always felt like she was being watched. At first, she shrugged it off, assuming that she was just imagining things. As she got older, however, the feeling only got worse. She began to feel as though she was never alone. She felt as though she had to look, feel, and be her best even when nobody was around because she always felt like someone was around. Arlene knew that it was ridiculous to think that anyone was watching her at all times. Perhaps it was paranoia, she thought. Perhaps it was egotism, her younger brother Joey offered.

"I don't know why I ever tell you anything," Arlene commented.

"Uh, because I'm your awesome and intelligent brother," Joey answered.

Arlene snorted, "Now who's being egotistical?"

Her brother smirked, "It runs in the family." Joey threw a grape in the air and tried to catch it, but it landed in his eye instead. Arlene tried not to laugh thinking that it would only encourage him. "Arlene, have you considered, you know, talking to a professional?"

"A professional what?" Arlene challenged.

"Well, you know, a professional... Jeez I don't know what they're called. The guys who talk to crazy people?"

"Exactly," Arlene countered. "The last thing I need is for everyone to think I'm insane. I have my whole life ahead of me, I'm not about to throw it away by being labeled as some crazy person that has no valuable input. I go see a psychiatrist and overnight I'll be hearing 'maybe you're just imagining things,' or 'be careful about taking Arlene seriously, she's crazy you know.'"

"I'd listen to you," Joey popped a grape into his mouth, legs hanging over the arm of the couch.

"You don't listen to me now. Like how many times have I told you to not put your shoes on the couch?"

"They're over the couch not on the couch you crazy woman."

Arlene sighed heavily.

"How about this," Joey offered. "I promise that no matter what, I won't think of you any more insane than I already think you are, and I won't stop listening to you more than usual."

"That's hardly an improvement nor is it inciting any confidence," Arlene admitted. Joey said something else, but Arlene's attention turned to the window facing the front door. "Did you hear that?"

"Hm? What? Hear what?" Joey asked.

"I thought I heard someone call my name. Maybe mom's home and needs help with the groceries." Arlene pressed her hands to the window and scanned the front yard, but there was no mom, no car, not even a casual jogger that the neighborhood had on occasion. Arlene shrugged. "Must have been hearing things."

She turned around to see Joey's wide eyes. Arlene returned the stare, raising an eyebrow. "What, Joey?"

"Do you usually hear voices?" Joey asked.

Arlene felt her face grow hot and she avoided her brother's accusing stare. "Whatever, sometimes. You're telling me you don't?"

"No," Joey turned his head left and right, keeping his attention to his sister. "How often do you hear voices?"

"Not often," Arlene crossed her arms, face flushed red. "Just you know, a couple times a week." She didn't mention that was the lower estimate. It happened much more often whenever she was stressed out.

Joey got up from the couch, walked to his sister, and put his hands on her shoulders. "Call somebody. Listen, Arlene? Are you listening? Frickin' call someone. Nip it in the bud, just call someone right now."

"Are you forgetting I only have my permit? Our parents aren't going to have the time to drive me to and from therapy or whatever. Besides, I'm fine. I have it under control."

Arlene convinced Joey to drop the subject. She never called anyone and she never told her parents. So what if she was hearing things sometimes, she knew other people that heard things sometimes. Arlene convinced herself that it was no big deal.

"Arlene."

Arlene's eyes shot open. It was the sleepiest part of the night and she was the only person awake in the house. She turned to pull the chain on her lamp. Her room was washed with a warm, yellow light. Arlene searched the room from the comfort of her bed for whoever called her name, but she was alone. Strange, it sounded like they said her name right in her ear. Maybe she dreamed it.

Arlene's eyes stopped at the window across the room. Her body shivered. Despite having never been afraid of the dark and seeing only blackness out the window, she couldn't stop thinking that someone was peering in at her. Arlene pulled the drapes over the window. She caught the eye of the posters of bands she enjoyed. Their printed eyes bothered her. Arlene couldn't ignore it, she took down each poster and set the paper face down. Satisfied, she curled up into her covers and fell asleep.

Class was the same every day. Arlene paid little attention to the lectures, but she could afford to. She wore the same old uniform and doodled the same old things while dreaming the same old daydreams. She imagined being in the music business. She wanted to find and promote the next greatest musicians. She imagined finding a group of amazing performers, unrealized and unorganized. They were her gem in a cornfield, the pearl in an oyster farm. She imagined training them, hyping them up, making them recognized, and most of all making a lot of money.

"Arlene."

Her spine straightened to attention, eyes forward. She realized it wasn't the professor since he was still droning on about derivatives. Arlene looked inconspicuously around to her classmates, but no one was paying her attention. Her eye briefly caught someone outside the window.

Arlene spun her head around to find no one at the window. Her face went hot. She felt stupid. Of course, there would be no one there, they were on the second floor.

Her heart froze in her chest, becoming petrified and feeling like a boulder pushing her lungs. She realized this was the first time she was ever seeing things. Was she going to continue seeing things? She thought about the wide-eyed stare Joey gave her a couple days prior. It was just one time, she told herself. This was the only time she ever thought she saw something that wasn't there. Lots of people have seen things out the corner of her eye before. It must have been a cloud hovering over the sun that tricked her eyes into thinking it was a person's shadow instead.

Days passed and Arlene forgot about the shadow and when she heard her name late at night. A while more passed and Arlene forgot about her conversation with her brother, but she still felt like she was being watched. Arlene didn't notice it, yet she would look out the window more frequently. She went on with her life and eventually got her driver's license.

"Why did you take your posters down?"

"Huh?" Arlene turned her attention to Joey who, as usual, walked into her room without knocking.

"Your posters. Why did you take them down?"

"Oh," Arlene forgot about the posters. She was too preoccupied with school and getting her license and… Other things. "Why does it matter?" Arlene replied.

"I mean I guess it doesn't, I was just curious," Joey muttered. Arlene shrugged. "Anyway," Joey swung the door open more. "Dad says to come down for dinner."

"What are we having?" Arlene asked.

"Food," Joey answered while being way too proud of himself. "It doesn't matter, we're eating it either way. Just get downstairs. Why are your drapes closed?"

"Are you gonna keep interrogating me?" Arlene challenged.

"It's just your window is always open, jeez. I'm just curious, stop being so sensitive over the dumbest stuff."

Joey turned to go back downstairs, leaving Arlene to herself. She leaned back in her desk-chair and groaned at the ceiling. "Dang it, Joey. Mind your own business."

Dinner was more silent than usual. Arlene noticed that her mom and dad weren't talking to each other. Did they have an argument? Their mom asked Joey and Arlene about school and if Arlene was happy about her new ticket to freedom. Joey ate and answered questions, unaware of the tension in the air. Their dad asked about Joey's drumming lessons and Arlene's applications for scholarships. Arlene didn't really need the money; her family was good for it. Still, she was over-qualified and winning scholarships looked good on paper. When dad asked about the scholarships, however, she saw her mother drop her arm on the table and roll her eyes. Arlene had never seen her mother act like that before, yet even then neither parent said a word about the issue between them.

Arlene took it upon herself to eavesdrop into her parent's room that night. The two took turns arguing in hushed tones.

"It doesn't matter that I make enough money to support us right now, we need to save money for Arlene and Joey to go to college," Her father growled.

"I told you I'm trying my best," Her mother whispered. "Stop pressuring me so hard, I'm doing everything I can."

"I just don't see what's taking so long. Suppose the kids find out your company laid you off, what will they think?"

Arlene's mother snapped at his comment, "It's been two weeks! The job market isn't like it was when we were kids, David."

"I don't want to hear your excuses, Hayley." David muttered.

"I'm not making excuses," Hayley's voice cracked as the words dripped out of her mouth like venom. "As my husband I would appreciate a little less criticism and a little more support."

Arlene had heard enough. With a light creak of the floorboards, Arlene retreated into her room. Her head was filled with nightmares she never thought she would have. She never had to worry about money or her family's stability. It had been constant since she could remember. She never heard her parents talking so bitterly to each other. She never thought for once in her life that they would ever have a reason to worry about money. Her thoughts spiraled to them all living in the street, hungry and homeless. As unlikely as it was, the sound of her parent's voices in her head kept convincing her that it was the most logical consequence.

"Arlene."

Arlene jolted awake. Even with her drapes closed, the weekend sunlight brightened her room. She could see everything in her room and there was no one in sight. She groaned irritably and threw the covers over her head as she flopped down onto the bed. Everything she found out the day before came rushing back to her. She closed her eyes as tight as she could, trying to convince herself that she dreamed it, but she knew better.

Arlene tossed the covers from her body and slumped to the edge of her bed, slipping her slippers on. She sat there dazed, reliving the facts and interactions of last night. She heard the sizzling of breakfast being made downstairs. Her father was most likely at work already, which meant that it was either Joey or their mother making breakfast. She hoped it was her mother, Joey always cooked everything too thoroughly. Arlene wondered if she should tell Joey what she heard. He was a jerk, but he was still a member of the family. Arlene figured he should be in on family issues. Still, what would be the easiest way of telling him?

Nearly an hour passed of Arlene sitting at the foot of her bed, gathering the strength to continue with her life. She heard Joey working on his drumming in his bedroom. He was starting to get pretty good, though Arlene still didn't appreciate the loud banging noises in the morning. She heard her mother call them down for breakfast.

As the three sat together and ate, Arlene noticed that her mother wasn't as talkative as she used to be. Joey was too busy stuffing his face to say anything. "So mom," Alene began. "How have you been?" It wasn't the most inventive way to start a conversation, but it was better than the sound of Joey's obnoxious chewing. Hayley turned her attention to Arlene. "I'm doing fine, sweetheart. How are you?"

Arlene couldn't tell her the truth. She tried frantically to think of something to say. She needed a topic they could roll with at least for the duration of the meal. "Well," She faltered. "There's a new boy in my math class."

"Oh?" Hayley asked. "Has he caught your eye?"

"You gotta crush on the new kid?" Joey asked with a mouth full of eggs.

Arlene ignored him. "I mean, he seems very smart, he has a quick wit, he's very practical," She commented.

"He's a complete bore," Joey chimed in.

"Do you know him too, Joey?" Hayley asked.

"Yeah, he's in my band class. He's such a snob and really full of himself."

Arlene started to regret choosing this topic. "No one asked for your approval, Joey," Arlene warned. Joey shrugged and went back to eating his food.

"What's this boy's name?" Hayley inquired.

Arlene shrugged, pretending that her cheeks weren't getting hot. "His name is Ryan," She confessed. "Ryan Dalkovich."

"Dalkovich, huh," Hayley suddenly went silent again. Arlene wondered if she said anything wrong.

"I think I might have met his father," Hayley admitted. "He's the new head of my advertising firm."

Arlene's face went a little pale. "I never met Ryan's dad," She quickly confessed. "But hey mom, this food is great."

"Thank you, honey," Hayley replied. The table fell silent again for the rest of the meal.

Arlene woke up in the middle of the night again, but this time it wasn't because of a voice. Instead, even though Arlene always felt like she was being watched, the feeling was overpowering that night. She was facing the wall, arms wrapped around her body pillow. She felt oddly wide awake. Arlene turned around when she noticed her window.

She kept the drapes closed, but they were open just enough for her to see that someone was standing on the tree outside her window, not moving, looking straight into her window.

Every muscle in her body froze. She thought of screaming, but then that would scare him off and no one would see him. She didn't know what to do, she just kept her eyes wide and her body still. He had binoculars over his eyes, wearing beige work pants and a brown jacket. He remained perfectly still. Could he not see that she was looking right at him? With all her lights off, he shouldn't be able to see inside her room at all. Arlene started to regain control of her body. She slowly, methodically slid off of her bed. The peeping Tom still didn't make a move. She moved in closer. He was looking right at her clear as crystal. She could make out his entire body except for his face. The binoculars were in the way.

Arlene snuck up to her window, her eyes fixated on the peeping Tom. She dove behind the curtain for a brief moment and pulled the drapes back to peer out the window.

He was gone.

There was no noise. There was no movement. Where he was before was just a branch and some leaves. They didn't even remotely resemble the peeping Tom.

Arlene closed off any crack there could be between her window and her. Her breathing hollowed. She no longer felt safe in her room. In a flash, she ran to the closest room with someone else in it. "Joey," Arlene whispered, her voice squeaking as her throat tried to make noise with the stone of fear in her chest.

Joey groaned and rolled over. "What is it? What's wrong?" He asked.

Arlene suddenly felt foolish, but she just couldn't bring herself to go back to her room. She looked over to Joey's window and quickly closed the curtains on it. Joey straightened up in his bed. "Arlene what the heck are you doing?"

"I think I saw someone spying on me through the window," She blurted. "Joey, can I please sleep in here with you?"

Joey was taken aback. At first, he didn't register her request. Slowly, he began to realize what she was proposing and what happened. "Did they break into the house?"

"No, they," Arlene tried to calm her breathing. "They were just staring, not moving. They just stared at me and they had binoculars and everything and now they're gone and I don't know where they went."

Joey rubbed his face with his hands. "Will it make you feel better to sleep in here with me? Shouldn't we call the police?"

"N-no," Arlene decided. "I just want to sleep somewhere safe."

Her brother let out a long sigh. He scooted to one end of his bed so she had room to push her way in. "We haven't slept in the same bed since we were kids."

"I know." Arlene's heart beat so hard that she could feel it hit her nightgown. Her stomach hurt. She didn't want to tell Joey that the man just disappeared when she peered out to look at him better. She was terrified that it was another hallucination. But she kept eye contact with him for what seemed like minutes. The trees and leaves around where he was didn't seem at all to resemble his shape or size. It was the perfect detailed image of a man holding binoculars while standing on the branch of a tree. Arlene didn't know what to think. She didn't know who to tell or even if she should tell anyone at all. Would everyone assume she was making it up?

Joey fell back to sleep immediately. Arlene spent the second night in a row contemplating the sudden changes she was undergoing in her life. She couldn't take it anymore. She had to talk to someone.

Arlene borrowed her mother's car to drive to a psychiatrist she found in the yellow pages. He seemed to have a decent reputation from what she could tell without asking people outright who she should go to. The visit was pricey, something Arlene wouldn't have considered before if she wasn't aware that her mother lost her job. Even so, she took the money from her allowance. This was something that had to be done.

The office was nicer than what she was expecting. It seemed like a regular health doctor's clinic. She didn't know what she was expecting. Arlene filled out the paperwork for the visit and waited. She kept bouncing her right knee while watching the clock tick away. When at last she was called, Arlene jumped from her seat and hurried inside the office. While she was in the office, she ended up waiting another five minutes before the psychiatrist finally made an appearance.

He wandered in, bent over a clipboard and flipping through some pages. He looked up to smile at her. "Arlene Silverman, is it?" He asked. "My name is doctor Jeremy Hughes. You can call me Hughes or Jeremy or whatever will make you feel most comfortable. Would you like something to drink before we start? I have some tea, hot chocolate or lemonade."

"No," Arlene faltered. "Thank you. But I'm fine."

The doctor sat on a chair across from her. He leaned back and set the clipboard on the desk behind him. "You were very vague in the paperwork. Is there anything you would like to let me know before we begin?"

"Doctor, I need you to tell me if I'm going crazy," Arlene demanded. "I've been seeing things and hearing things that aren't there. I always feel like I'm being watched. Every time I look outside I panic a little bit."

"Oh?" Hughes straightened himself. "Would you feel more comfortable if I turned on the lights and closed the curtain?" He asked, gesturing to the window.

Arlene didn't honestly notice it before, but she was grateful that doctor Hughes offered to close it. She didn't want a repeat of last night. "Please," She requested.

The doctor got up and turned on the light to the room before closing the blue curtains over the window displaying the outside world. Oddly enough, when Arlene felt closed-in as they were then, she felt calmer. The doctor seemed sincere and she started to understand all the amazing reviews she heard. He sat back down and crossed his legs. "I apologize for interrupting, please continue."

Arlene let out a deep breath. "I always feel like I'm never alone. It's like eyes are watching me everywhere. Before it was just a small annoyance but lately things are getting out of control."

"How so?" Hughes asked.

Arlene explained the experience last night with the peeping Tom. She talked about her conversation with her brother along with every other instance she can remember where she either saw someone out of a window or heard someone calling her name. "It's like I'm living my life in a coma and every whisper in my ear is like someone from the real world trying to call me awake, but I know how ridiculous that is."

"Mmmh," The doctor nodded his head and closed his eyes. He

contemplated and ruminated about every word she said to him. "And you are completely certain the man you saw out your window last night was a hallucination?"

"It seemed so real," Arlene confessed. "But it had to be. No man could climb down the tree so quietly or so quickly. Even as I was staring at him, he seemed too still to be human."

"Hmm," Hughes opened his eyes and sat there, thumb to his lip, eyes glued to the closed window. Arlene felt her heartbeat quicken. "So what do you think, doctor? Have I lost my mind?"

The doctor's gentle caramel eyes locked on to Arlene's steel-gray stare. "No, I do not think you lost your mind, Arlene. Even people who have never experienced hallucinations before can often develop them during times of stress. It is not so uncommon nor is it a sign of insanity. Forget what the movies tell you, gaining these symptoms are not an automatic ticket to madness. Arlene, you seem very aware of what these visions are. You have explained to me some symptoms of a number of mental illnesses, but even if you had a mental illness, you are no crazier than anyone else in this room, or this office, or this town. You are experiencing paranoia and hallucinations. If you like we can work together to get to the bottom of it, but please keep in mind that there is nothing to be ashamed or afraid of."

Arlene absorbed the doctor's words. She nodded and fell silent, thinking about what her symptoms could mean. "If anyone ever finds out that I hallucinate, no one will ever believe what I have to say."

"I certainly would," Hughes countered. "Just because you can at times experience mirages doesn't mean your feelings and opinions are any less valid. Just try to surround yourself with people who will understand that."

Somehow, Hughes' attitude and words towards the news helped her calm down. Arlene felt better. "Should I tell anyone else?"

"Don't feel obligated to," Jeremy assured her. "If you feel ready to tell anyone then by all means. But don't force yourself to do something that you don't feel ready to do."

Arlene headed home feeling a lot more confident. She wasn't sure how the doctor was able to relax her so flawlessly but she felt like he was worth the outrageous cost. She wasn't gone for long. Arlene parked her mother's car and went back upstairs to try and enjoy the last of her weekend.

When she got into her room, her voice caught in her throat. The drapes to her window were wide open. 'Who's been in my room?' She thought. Arlene closed the window and looked around some of the most important items in her room to make sure everything was in its place. Satisfied that at least nothing else had been tampered with, Arlene closed the door to her room and buried her face into her pillows.

She heard her door open. Without looking she said, "What is it, Joey?"

Joey's voice responded, "Hey do you think you can drive me to this Battle of the Bands concert happening at the Brew n' Beats?"

"When?" Arlene asked.

"Tonight, at seven. I'll treat you to a coffee there if you do."

Arlene turned her head to stare at her brother through the pillow. "Have you been coming into my room while I'm gone?"

"What? No," Joey said.

Arlene didn't believe him. "My curtain was wide open when I came in. I had it closed before I left."

"I don't know what to tell you sister," Joey replied. "I've been trying to catch up on homework so I could go to the concert."

'What a lame alibi,' Arlene thought. Still, she decided to drop the subject. With a deep sigh, she sat up. "Hey, come in and close the door. There's something I better tell you."

"Ooooooookaaaaaay?" Joey closed the door. He kept a wide distance between him and his older sister in case she was planning something sinister.

Arlene thought a moment about what the doctor said. "Joey, you said that if I went crazy you would still trust me if I told you something, right?"

"Is this a test?" Joey raised an eyebrow.

"Just answer the question," Arlene retorted.

"I mean, sure," Joey replied. "I believed you about the peeping Tom last night, didn't I?"

He had her there. Joey never once mocked her or questioned her about the experience. He only first trusted her that she saw someone and then didn't follow up on questions when she claimed she was seeing things but wanted to sleep with her brother anyway. He just looked after her like a good brother.

"I went to see a psychiatrist today," She confessed. Joey only nodded. "I'm experiencing hallucinations and paranoia. I think maybe it could be something like schizophrenia, but the doctor said it's too soon to know for sure what it is. I'm planning on seeing him once a week."

"Okay," Joey nodded more. "So, you're getting help, huh? He's not gonna tie you and lock you up like you thought?"

"I guess it isn't as bad as I made it out to be," Arlene admitted. "But there's something else. A couple nights ago I overheard mom and dad talking. Did you notice that mom hasn't gone to work recently? She got fired. Dad is pretty upset about it."

Joey shrugged it off and rubbed his arm. "Dad is always upset about something."

"Yeah but not at mom. It was, I don't know, bizarre."

"Are you telling me this because you thought I wouldn't believe you that our parents have been fighting? My room is right across from theirs. They fight occasionally at night about money or people they hire or even about us. Trust me, everything is going to be fine. Mom will find another job soon enough and things will go back to normal."

Arlene didn't know whether to be relieved or perturbed that her brother seemed to know the whole situation. On the one hand, it wasn't anything new or groundbreaking for the family. On the other hand, it would mean that Arlene was truly the one always out of the loop. "Why didn't you ever tell me that they argue like that?" She demanded.

"You've always been kind of a worrier. I didn't want to get you all worked up over nothing."

Arlene huffed, "What, you never got worried about it?"

Joey shrugged, "Not really. I mean, people argue. That's just life. Besides, even in the worst situation I could think of I knew I had my older sister around." He gave her a smirk.

Arlene raised an eyebrow. "Are you trying to be funny?"

Joey laughed. "No but seriously. You're always able to keep it together, you know? I look up to you or whatever."

"You look up to me or whatever," Arlene parroted.

Joey's face grew red. "You're gonna make something of yourself is all. The whole family knows it. Dad is convinced I'll be the first drop-out in the family."

Arlene straightened her back. She felt like the mood shifted from casual to serious confession time. "Joey, you're not any less smart than I am. You're just smart about different things."

"Thanks for the confidence," Joey muttered.

"No seriously," Arlene stood up to stand eye-level to her brother. "We're different in a lot of ways. I'm more uptight and you're more carefree. I try to get everything done right away and you take your time. I stay home or at school and you like to spend time with friends and at local concerts. Even still, none of us are any better or worse than the other. We're both driven, we're both competitive, and we both care about our family. Even if you did drop out, and it wouldn't be because you couldn't make it but because you wanted to, that doesn't change the fact that you're a really smart guy. You're gonna make something of yourself too, you know. It doesn't matter what dad thinks."

Joey couldn't make eye contact with her. He rubbed at his arm and cleared his throat. "Thanks, Arlene. That's um. That's pretty cool of you to say."

After a few minutes of bonding, Joey left Arlene to do her homework and start the day. After their talk, Arlene felt a lot better. On the one hand, she was exposed to the revelation that their father didn't have high hopes for Joey, which admittedly left Arlene's blood to boil. On the other hand, the two of them had each other. Even if their family did fall apart, she had no doubt that she could count on Joey to stick around. It was just the feeling she needed.

Arlene drove Joey to see the concert at the local coffee shop. He bought her a coffee as promised and she stayed longer than she normally would. As much as she dreamed of being a manager in the music business, she always felt awkward being in the crowd. It was loud and people were bumping into each other and she didn't know anyone, but she enjoyed listening to the first couple bands as she sipped her coffee and spent some time with her brother. One of Joey's friends said they would drive him home so she had a chance to leave early enough to get a good night's sleep before class the next day.

"Arlene."

Her eyes shot awake. She felt groggier than before, perhaps due to the coffee. Arlene didn't have much time to register her surroundings before noticing that, once again, the drapes were wide open. Blocking the window was a human-shaped figure, eyes strangely illuminated though the body remained veiled by the darkness.

37

Arlene's heart froze. Her entire body tingled and she couldn't move. The figure wasn't on the tree outside. The dark figure staring at her, unblinking, was just two feet from her bed. Inside. The cool breeze of the open window blew in her face.

She screamed.

Leaves rustled outside and everything went black. Arlene realized that her eyes were closed and she shot up in bed. She scanned around the pitch-black room before fumbling for her desk lamp. With relief, no one was in the room with her. Even more importantly, the drapes were closed. Still, what was that rustling before? It could have been a squirrel, but she couldn't be satisfied until she knew for sure. Arlene braved her bedroom window and threw open the curtain. There was sudden movement below near their yard fence. Arlene gripped the curtain as she watched a human-sized figure retreat into the hedge and climb over their fence.

Arlene stood in place, petrified at what she witnessed. The peeping Tom. She couldn't believe it, he was real. Or was this another hallucination?

No, this was different. She knew what she saw this time. Arlene hurried to her brother's room. "Joey," She cried. "Joey it's the peeping Tom again, he was just here!"

Joey groaned. Arlene shook him awake and he groaned some more. "Whatever it is tell me tomorrow," he whined.

"Joey," Arlene's voice squeaked. She felt her eyes water. Her hands were shaking. "It's the peeping Tom."

Her brother rubbed his face with his hands to force himself awake. "Is he still around?"

"No, he hopped the fence but he was here," Arlene cried.

Joey scooted and patted next to him on the bed. "Then you're safe now. Get some sleep and we'll talk about it in the morning." He mumbled the last of his statement before falling back asleep. Arlene took the time to breathe and managed to relax a little. He was right, the stalker was gone now. She closed the drapes of Joey's window, closed his door and scooted into bed again. It took nearly an hour for her to fall back asleep. She envied her brother. He could sleep through anything.

The following morning, Arlene explained to Joey what happened last night. As she explained it, however, she started to doubt herself. "Maybe it was a hallucination," She admitted.

"I don't think it was," Joey countered. His voice sounded bitter. He crossed his arms and lowered his head.

"No, it had to be," Arlene reasoned. "My drapes were closed. What could a peeping Tom expect to achieve if he can't see me?"

"Maybe," Joey's voice went quieter. "He was trying to break in."

Arlene's body jumped as a chill surged through her nerves. "Why," She couldn't finish her question.

"I don't know, but we should tell mom and dad. Or the police."

"No," Arlene shook her head. "No, we can't do that. Even if they believed me, what if I imagined all of it? I could get in a lot of trouble."

Joey fell silent.

"Kids, breakfast!" Hayley called up to them. "You better be ready for school!"

It was painfully difficult to pay attention to the professor in class. She pretty much understood what he was explaining anyway, but Arlene wished she could just shut off her brain and listen for a little while. She made Joey promise to not tell anyone she was seeing and hearing things, but her nerves were still on-edge. She jumped when she felt something touch her arm.

Arlene turned to see that the girl next sitting behind her was trying to hand her a note. She didn't pass notes in class, but this one was a folded piece of paper that read 'To Arlene' on the front. Curiously, she took the paper and kept looking forward to make sure the professor wasn't paying attention. He either never did or he never cared.

She opened the letter.

'Let's talk during passing. Ryan.'

Arlene's eyes widened; her cheeks ignited into flame. She looked around to see if she could catch his eye. Ryan sat in the center of the classroom. He was staring right at her. Arlene ran her fingernails through her hair and gave him a nod. He smirked and looked back down at his desk.

All previous thoughts left Arlene's mind. Now all she could think about was how she was about to have a one-on-one conversation with Ryan Dalkovich.

He was waiting for her when she walked out of class. They stood in a less crowded hallway. "So, I heard you had a crush on me," Ryan blurted. She stood there, mouth agape, unable to think of how to respond. "Sorry, it's cool. I just wanted to tell you that I like you too," he admitted. Arlene's spirit ascended to space and floated back down to her living body so fast that she nearly lost track of time or where she was.

"You do?" Was her response.

Ryan chuckled and scratched at his cheek. "Sorry, I'm not too great at subtlety. I'd rather be straightforward. Do you not like me back?"

"No, I do," Arlene blurted. Her face was so hot she thought she was going to faint. "I'm just surprised is all. How did you know I liked you?"

"Oh, well," Ryan blushed back. "I shouldn't reveal my source. Confidentiality and all that," He joked. "So, what do you think about maybe going to see a movie with me next Saturday? Would that be cool?"

"So cool," Arlene cleared her throat and shifted the weight in her feet. She kept running her fingertips through her pixie-short hair. She wished then that she could tolerate her hair to be long enough to tuck behind her ear. She read somewhere that guys generally liked when girls did that. "Um, uh, so maybe I can give you my address and you could pick me up?"

"You live over on Ivy Oak road, right? One of your brother's friends mentioned that once."

"Yeah, Joey has friends over often."

"You think he would have friends over Saturday?" Ryan asked.

"Naw," She shrugged. "Joey spends most weekends watching concerts or hanging out with his friends."

"Arlene."

Arlene's eyes flicked towards where she thought she heard her name. She found herself looking out the window. "Ah, anyway. We should get to class. Talk to you later?"

Ryan smirked. "Absolutely."

The rest of Arlene's day happened in the clouds. On the way home, she told Joey the great news.

"He doesn't deserve you, honestly."

Arlene laughed, "I know you don't like him but he's a good guy. He's driven and persistent. He wants to be a businessman like his dad."

"Yeah but I think he's too driven and persistent. In gym and in band he always has this I-can-get-whatever-I-want attitude. He thinks that since his father is worth a damn that automatically means that he is, too. I don't know I just don't like him."

"Well, if we're going to start dating then you have to be on your best behavior."

Joey laughed and gently nudged his sister. "Good luck with that."

The next couple days and nights went on normally. Arlene wondered if maybe since she wasn't stressed anymore that it was why the hallucinations stopped. She still always felt like she was being watched, but that feeling started becoming so normal that Arlene never paid much attention to it. Joey seemed a little less laid back. She wondered if he wasn't feeling well, but she also didn't want to get too much into his business. He would come to her if he needed her, she thought.

The night before Saturday, Arlene had a hard time sleeping. She was so excited for her date that it took longer than usual for her to settle down. She looked up at her posters, wondering what music Ryan liked. What sort of books did he like to read? Was he more of a taco person or did he prefer burgers? Her daydreaming slowly settled into actual dreams as her eyes drifted closed and her breathing paced itself through the night.

"Arlene."

A sharp inhale and a tingling all over her body caused Arlene to shudder. She knew that as soon as she opened her eyes, she was going to see something horrifying. She knew that as soon as she opened her eyes, she would see the window open and she would see a man there. She knew that as soon as she opened her eyes she would be hallucinating and scare herself so much that she would sleep in Joey's room. She opened them anyway.

Arlene laid there for a few moments. There was no open window, no man in her room, and no shadowy figures. All she witnessed was sequential flashes of red and blue. She heard noises outside. Cautiously, Arlene slipped on her slippers and snuck to the curtain. Her fingers barely made contact with the curtain as she peeked through.

There was a police car outside. They were putting someone in the back. Both her parents were talking to one of the officers. Joey was there, arms crossed, watching the other officers apprehend the mystery person. Arlene pulled the curtains back more. He looked up to her room and seeing her awake hurried inside. She felt her heart start to race. She thought about doing a hundred different things but could manage only to stand there and wait for her brother.

Joey opened her door and hurried into her room. "You were right," He told her.

Arlene blinked. "Right about what?"

"The peeping Tom."

She felt her legs go weak. She sat on her desk-chair.

"I'm sorry, Arlene. It was Ryan."

Arlene looked up to Joey, his image flashing in the red and blue lights. She searched for any sign of humor. She desperately explored every twitch in his face for proof that he was joking.

"He came in with a crowbar. I think he was planning on breaking into your room. He may have been stalking you for a while."

"So those times I saw someone out my window," Arlene whispered.

"Who knows how long he's been coming by. I can't tell you how much of it was fake and how much was real but I wasn't about to take the chance."

Arlene blinked. "You called the police?"

"I told them there was a guy wandering the neighborhood at night trying to sneak into buildings. I didn't know for sure if it would be true, and I never told them it was you who saw them. But I had to say something to make sure they started searching around. I stayed up almost every night since last weekend. I even started mistaking shadows made by squirrels and raccoons for the stalker, but once I saw him sneaking over to the tree by your window, I called the police instantly."

"You believed me the whole time, even when I wasn't sure I believed myself. You maybe saved my life, Joey."

"At the very least I stopped a creep from creeping on my sister. I'm sorry it was the Ryan guy you liked so much. I always had a bad feeling about him."

Arlene looked down at the floor. She took some time to find the words. "What do we do now?"

"I don't know about you," Joey replied. "But I'm going to bed."

Arlene felt her breathing falter. "And after that? What about school? What if everyone finds out about this? What if they find out about my paranoia or my hallucinations? What if nobody will believe me about what happened?"

"I'm here for you, sis," Joey assured her. "Let's just take everything as it comes one day at a time, okay? Things will go back to normal eventually."

Arlene wasn't so sure. It was impossible to fall back asleep, but she managed somehow. The following week, classmates asked and wondered about Ryan. Luckily, no one seemed to catch wind that Arlene was involved at all. She continued to go to counseling once a week, even when life was ultimately just fine, Arlene found comfort in talking to Dr. Hughes. As promised, Joey remained by her side. She never got over always feeling like she was being watched, but every time she heard her name from then on, she would always find the person saying it.

THE PERFORMANCE

When the heat of the closest star is snuffed out and the mirage of the sky fades away, demons of the night emerge from their hiding corners. Shrouded images stretch their long fingers and clutch at the remains of the light, quieting candles and silencing sounds. When they think no one is looking, they sway and weave between shadows, whispering late night thoughts into your ear. Closing your eyes, you open the curtains for the dream demons to perform. Some entice you with colors and feelings while others stage a show so vague that you wake the next morning unphased. One demon, however, never fails to affect you with its's performance.

The nightmare demon composes a symphony in your honor. It pulls the darkness from your mind and commissions your fears as the thespians. It writes the script with screams from your throat and water from your eyes. Your memories are inspiration and your anxiety its climax. It builds on the library you've unknowingly given it. The nightmare demon tugs at the strings you've desperately hidden.

As the play unfolds, your screams are applause. Your cold sweat are the roses laid on the stage. Like any good performance, it leaves you thinking. You wake from the stage different than before. The nightmare demon bows reverently, promising you an encore.

ELOISE

There are so many differences between humans. They can look different, act differently, and think differently. Even if two humans act the same, it can often be for different motives. People like and dislike different things and interpret the world in different ways. Even so, there are things that most humans have in common. Humans need fresh air. Humans need to eat and drink. Humans need communication, a level of independence and most of all, in Eloise's opinion, love.

It was almost lights out, time to get the medicine. Eloise Bandit worked full time at the asylum. She was supposed to stay at least a little bit detached from them in order to keep objective over what the patient needed, yet she found herself adoring them all like family. She wasn't the only one with this problem. Despite all the awful rumors and mistreatment of patients that asylums often had, the owner of this particular building preferred results to revenue. Eloise enjoyed her coworkers. Well, most of them. She cared deeply for the patients as she worked on their exercises, bathed them, clothed them, played card games and listened to the radio with them.

Occasionally throughout the day, she had to go to a more secluded wing for a patient she took special care for. This resident was very young and she couldn't help but adore the boy on his good days, however his manic episodes were so severe that the facility had to cut his care staff to three people. Eloise cared for him during most night shifts, replaced only on her days off. She never met the person that relieved her. It could be the facility head for all she knew, but so long as Chase was getting the help that he needed, she didn't have much reason to know.

It was nearly the end of her shift and the last thing she did was put him to sleep. None of his family came to visit today, which wasn't too odd since they all were busy with their own lives. Chase's mother and older brother visited nearly three times a week, but never on the same day. Sometimes his aunt visited when her travels brought her that way. His father came only once a year, on Chase's birthday. Eloise could tell they all loved him. Part of her job was to learn how each patient communicated. She wished she could explain to his family, but it was so hinged on certain special cues that it would take months to understand even if she did tell them. Still, it was good of them to come over as much as they did. Few patients got visits from anyone.

As Eloise walked towards his room, she could hear him talking.

"There is a fine young man who lives right around the corner. Would you like more cream?"

Eloise peered into his room and watched as he poured imaginary cream into an imaginary cup. "He has a father with a coffee bean business and he sent his dear son over to bring me some," he continued.

Eloise watched Chase lean forward and nod his head. After a few seconds of silence, he sat up straight and laughed.

"Haha, oh Maggie, you and your tea."

Chase started humming a tune that Eloise would sometimes sing. She continued to spy on him through the one-way window and watched him rock back and forth, humming the song and sipping into an imaginary cup. He had almost this exact same conversation every day. Every worker that came to the intensive care unit knew about Chase's coffee and how it came from a boy down the corner. Eloise knew he saw himself as older and that he spoke to his imaginary friends Wiggy and Maggie. The way Chase spoke to them when he was alone made him sound like how Eloise's own father spoke from time to time.

"Ah, oh yes. I have been doing quite fine. My roses are growing quite beautifully, and I managed to fix that darn washing machine…" Eloise took a deep breath. Chase was using the washing machine story again. That meant a bad day. Eloise held the needle close to her and unlocked the door.

"Go away! Can't you see I'm in the middle of having coffee?!"

Eloise slowly opened the door, speaking as calmly and sweetly as she could to the young 16-year-old boy, "It's just me Chase, Eloise, it's alright…"

"No, what have you done?!"

"It's time for your medicine Chase, let's get it done quickly now and I can let you get back to your tea party," She urged, giving him a reassuring smile.

"Aah! No, stay away!" Chase scooted back up to the farthest corner from the door and slowly started to pick himself up off the floor. "No! What was that?! Who are these people?!"

"Please Chase, we go through this every day." The nurse closed the door behind her and eked a little closer to the young black-haired boy. His eyes darted around the room. They were such a gorgeous blue color, but they were dulled from lack of sleep and puffed red from Chase's crying episodes.

"Back away!" Chase's voice was a high screech as he clawed at the wall and thrashed around, hitting his arms and legs and throwing his body at the padded corner. Eloise was slow, trying to speak through him calmly, but she couldn't hear herself think through the screaming. She grabbed his wrist, but he thrashed it away. Eloise put the needle in her pocket to get both his arms. If only she could just get him to sit still for six seconds...

Finally, Eloise got both his hands and pulled off the cap of his medicine with a free hand. She moved the needle to his arm once she found the vein. "There," she sighed.

"Demons from behind, demons..." Chase chanted before he started to loosen up. Once he was limp, Eloise moved him to his bed. The drug took effect quickly, Chase no longer resisted. She fluffed his pillow and put the blanket over him. He liked to sleep in his clothes, so the morning guy would just put fresh new pajamas on him every morning. That was good, since Eloise liked Chase being comfortable. "They are everything," Eloise heard Chase mutter. "The bathroom," and then a few more utterances. She knew Chase didn't have to use the bathroom, since she took him to go a little over an hour ago. Come to think of it, Chase mentioned the bathroom a lot and it had her curious. Just as often, Chase would repeat the words 'broken door' as well. Maybe it meant something. She was sure it had to. Chase never said anything that didn't mean something to him.

As for now, Chase was fast asleep in bed. She stroked the bangs off his forehead to soothe him. "You're a very special kid, Chase. I hope somewhere in there you know that you're loved very much." Eloise got up and closed the door behind her, locking it. She made her way to the offices where she could change out of her work clothes, clock out and go home.

Eloise returned to her small one-bedroom home in the suburbs. Half the furniture was gone. The only sounds that greeted her were the groaning of the hardwood floor and the screaming of her two cats. "I know you're hungry," She called to them. The calico and the black cat ran up to her and made sure to always be right under her feet the entire time she served up their dinner. Eloise didn't feel like cooking for herself so instead grabbed a few miscellaneous vegetables. She turned on the radio to listen to her show as she ate. Once her show was over, she turned the dial off and went to her room to put on her nightgown. The cats followed her in the room. The calico hid under the bed while the black cat demanded her attention. Eloise scratched his ear. "Chico's such a pretty boy," She praised. Once she settled into the bed too big for one person, both cats nestled beside her. The calico started kneading Eloise's chest. "Ow, Annie, stop clawing me there." Eloise pet them both absentmindedly before she fell asleep.

Like every night, she thought of the patients in the asylum. She felt bad for them, thinking about how uncomfortable the beds must be and how awful it would feel if she were in their position. Eloise didn't have the best life, but she could afford her house, barely, and go out whenever she wanted. She had two cats and a nice bed and she could prepare anything she wanted to eat. She could listen to her shows on the radio. She felt the worst about Chase. His mind was such a landmine of horrors. She always wished before bed that she could do something for him. She turned her head to the empty side of the bed. Sometimes life just wasn't fair.

Eloise woke up like every other morning. She went on her normal routine, but as she walked to the grocery store to purchase more cat food, she saw a familiar face that she didn't expect to see outside of work. "Skipper?"

The young man in question turned and smiled to her. "Miss Bandit, good morning," He chimed. His familiar long black hair was tied back into a ponytail. His sky-blue eyes were much livelier than his younger brother's.

Eloise brightened at the sight of him. "Skip, it's good to see you. Do you live around here? I thought you lived further downtown."

"I did," Skip explained. "I just moved here so I could be closer to my little brother. My next customer is closer as well."

It occurred to Eloise that she didn't know much about Chase's family. Every time anyone came to visit, the conversation was always centered around Chase. "I don't know if I know what you do for work," She admitted.

"Have I never told you?" Skip's eyebrows raised and he smiled a bit wider. "I am an interior designer."

"I've heard of that before. What do you do?" Eloise asked.

"People employ me to improve the decor of their homes. Sometimes I'll be working on something else like an office."

"Oh," Eloise offered.

Skip picked up on Eloise's confusion. "It's a very new field of business. You should watch me work sometime. My newest clients want me to help expand their home. The man was referred to me by my mother, of all people."

"Expanding it," Eloise thought out loud. She thought of her own home and how empty it felt recently. "Could you also reduce the feeling of a house?"

Skip shrugged, "No one has asked me to before but I could try. Why do you ask? Are you in need of some interior design?"

"I may be," Eloise muttered. "I'm sorry to cut our meeting short, but I have to rush my groceries home before I go to work."

"I can take you," Skip offered.

"How would I get home if you take me?" Eloise questioned.

"I could take you home, too," Skip replied. "I could take you to work, visit my brother for a little bit before I go, and then drive back to pick you up."

"It seems like a lot of trouble for you," Eloise tucked her curly red hair behind her ear.

"It's no trouble at all," Skip assured her. "I would like nothing more than to be able to spend some time with you and my brother," He added as an afterthought.

"Well," Eloise's eyes trailed towards the parking lot. "If you're sure that's what you want."

Skip and Eloise got her car and her groceries home before they headed towards the asylum. The first few minutes was filled with the background comfort of the radio. Eloise made an attempt to break the tension. "Have you ever heard of Dragnet?"

"I watch the show sometimes," Skip admitted.

"I have listened to it for years," Eloise responded. "I listen to it every week."

"You really like those radio shows, huh?"

"I don't even own a television," Eloise confirmed. "I'm not sure, it could be that I spent so much time listening to the radio shows with my mother that watching television doesn't appeal to me."

"I'm surprised they still play the radio shows."

"Gunsmoke is still airing new episodes," Eloise muttered defensively.

"Sure, but for how much longer? Everything is going to television these days," Skip countered. He took a glance at Eloise's dejected expression. "I'm sorry," He offered. "Those shows mean a lot to you, do they?"

"A little," Eloise admitted.

There was a bit more silence. "How is my brother doing?"

Eloise straightened up in her chair. "He's doing better. His medication seems to help him. He's more coherent throughout the day than before."

"Good," Skip sighed. "I was getting worried since my father tried to get electroshock therapy approved."

"Actually," Eloise admitted. "He tried really hard to have us do a lobotomy first. Our head doctors had to tell him almost in unison that nobody uses that treatment anymore. Then he tried to get us to approve electroshock therapy."

"If I didn't know any better, I would think my father would just prefer my brother to be dead," Skipper grumbled bitterly.

"I'm confident that isn't the case," Eloise tried to reassure him. "Chase, he's trying to pull through. He just has a lot of demons within him."

Skipper kept his eyes on the road. "I think we all have demons within us, Eloise. Who you are as a person depends a lot on how you choose to react to them."

Eloise felt a chill up her spine. "Please don't talk like that. If my mother were alive she would consider your words to be blasphemous, and it's just scary to think about."

"Sorry, again," Skip sighed. "I know you care about Chase a lot. You should have seen him when he was a kid. He was just, you know, a normal little boy. Then around the time he turned seven or eight he just..." Skip fell silent. Eloise's heart went out to him. "I just wish I could do something more."

Eloise looked ahead and smiled softly. "You make a world of a difference coming to see him so often."

"Well to be honest Eloise, he's not the only person I go to see."

Eloise turned to look to him. The car turned into the parking lot and Skip turned off the ignition. "I just want to let you know Eloise, you can come to me if you ever need anything."

Her already red face glowed at his offer. It was instantly met with a deep sigh. "Skip, you're a really nice guy. I'm afraid it wouldn't be right for me to seek company from a patient's relative, it just doesn't seem proper."

Skip lowered his head. "I would hate to make you feel uncomfortable." He got out of the car and opened the door for her. They both entered the asylum.

While walking down the hallway, a brown-eyed red-headed man was storming their way. Eloise recognized him instantly as the day worker who also took care of Chase. "Rory, where are you going so quickly?" She called out to him.

"I'm going home. I can't stand another minute around that woman."

"What woman," Skip inquired.

Rory turned to look Skip square in the eye. "Your insufferable mother, that's who. Good day to you both." Without another word, Rory stormed out of the building. Eloise and Skip looked to each other.

"My mother is still here? She never stays around this late, and never on a Wednesday. I better hide for now."

"What for?" Eloise asked.

Skip hurried behind a corner to wait. "Trust me Eloise, you don't want the two of us in the same room. I can stand my mother less than I can stand my father, and the only endearing feelings I have with him is that we're family. I hate to ask this of you, but if you could try to get her out as fast as you can I would be much obliged."

Eloise pursed her lips together and shrugged. "Alright Skip, I'll do what I can." She hoped that Rory didn't leave Chase alone with her, but then again, she expected very little of the day worker. He was always so surly and not friendly to any of his clients. It was a wonder why Chase seemed to like him. Eloise heard Chase screaming from down the hall. Eloise's heart jumped and she sprinted so fast that she had little time to think. She heard his mother wailing at him, saying things that didn't register in Eloise's mind. All that mattered at the moment was that Chase was upset and screaming his loudest. Other doctors hurried to the door, but Eloise was the first one there. She threw it open to see the mother forcing something down Chase's throat. She hovered over him and forced his mouth open, pouring something in which she kept in a vile. "What are you doing," Eloise cried before pushing the woman off of Chase. The vile flew out of her hand and shattered against a wall. "Get away from him," Eloise screamed.

"I am his mother," She reminded Eloise. "I have done nothing wrong."

Chase kept screaming, clutching his neck, eyes rolled back. Eloise's body quivered with rage and fear. "What did you give him?!"

The doctors rushed in to take Chase back into his room and began to escort Chase's mother out of the building. "Wait, what did you give him," Eloise screamed again. Her coworkers had to hold her back as she desperately demanded to know. She kept screaming at the woman that eventually faded from sight. No one would let her go into Chase's room until she calmed down. A doctor was the only person left in Chase's room to look over his vitals to make sure he hadn't been poisoned. Eloise urged the doctors that Chase should be taken to a hospital to extract whatever it was. They ignored her request, undoubtedly afraid of the ramifications of the law. 'Just wait to see what happens,' They told her. Skip hurried to Eloise to be caught up on what happened.

The doctor left Chase. Chase calmed down. Eloise and Skip listened in from outside to see if Chase would start talking to Maggie and Wiggy again. "Any idea of what your mother was trying to do?" Eloise whispered.

"The one thing I could always say about my mother was that she always loved Chase. I was always afraid something like this would happen."

Eloise turned to Skip. "Why?"

"Before we managed to get Chase here, our mother tried to exorcize the demon out of him. She was convinced that the devil himself was what was influencing him. Aunt Grace stopped everything before it got too out of hand. I hoped mom would have given up on it."

"But it's been five years since Chase was admitted here. Do you think she was trying some weird exorcism? Why would she choose now after so long?"

"I don't know," Skip shook his head. "It could have nothing to do with that. That's just my thought." He sighed and removed himself from the wall by Chase's door. "Maybe I shouldn't see him today, he's had enough family meetings for one afternoon."

"Oh no, he'd be happy to see you," Eloise assured him.

"No, I don't want to risk making things worse. What time do you leave work?"

"Ten," Eloise surrendered.

Skip gave her a nod, "Then I'll come back to take you home. I deeply apologize for all the trouble my family has given you.

"You and Chase are no trouble at all," Eloise smiled. "I enjoy your company. I'm only sorry there isn't more I can do."

"You are more help than you think. Thanks again, I'll see you tonight." Skip turned to see himself out. Eloise watched him go until he turned a corner towards the exit. She sighed.

"There is a fine young man who lives right around the corner. Would you like more cream?"

Eloise perked and spied on Chase through the window. He was rocking back and forth. "He has a father with a coffee bean business and he sent his dear son over to bring me some," he continued.

She could hear the tears he fought back as he spoke.

"Haha, oh Maggie, you and your tea."

Eloise bit her lower lip, her hand clutching to her chest, forcing the broken pieces of her heart to stay together. Her hand opened the door. Her legs pushed her into the room. Chase flinched but otherwise kept rocking. His face was red, puffy and wet. Eloise closed the door and sat down, her back leaning against it. This was dangerous. Patients could snap at any minute and attack the caretakers. Eloise being the only female caretaker, she was most commonly targeted with very crude behavior from several patients. However, knowing the danger, Eloise remained calm. She moved only to rub her eyes when the tears blurred her vision.

"No, no," Chase muttered. "Bathroom, the bathroom, broken door. It's broken. You idiot." He rocked more violently, shaking his head and keeping his focus on a fixed part of the wall. Eloise tried to think of something she could do.

She was quiet and out-of-tune, her voice cracking. But after a few seconds of her song, Chase's rocking was less intense. Eloise got louder. She hummed the familiar tune she always did when she wandered around the hallways. His heaving breaths and muttering quieted down. His rocking continued to calm down. Eloise continued the tune. Chase started to hum with her.

Eloise was so shocked that she nearly stopped. She kept up with Chase as he hummed the tune and closed his eyes, resting his chin on his knees. Eloise lost track of time. She hummed with the boy for what felt like an hour. She had to go see her other patients. She was starting to worry that someone would come looking for her and frighten Chase all over again. At last she noticed that Chase stopped. He fell asleep as he was curled up in a corner.

A few moments of stillness passed before Eloise stood to tuck Chase in bed. She continued the tune for him, softly and sweetly. She kept it up until she was out in the hallway. She closed the door behind her.

Chase was the last patient she visited during lights out. She had to have him take his medicine. She got the needle ready, but to her surprise he was still fast asleep. Eloise did her best to materialize into the room and float to the bed like a passing spirit. She wanted no sound to enter the chamber. She forbade any whisper and pleaded to her drumming heart. She took breaths sparingly. Eloise inserted the needle, extracting it as quickly as allowed. Once her task was complete, she brushed the hair from his eyes and wished him a silent goodnight.

"Is he okay?" Skip asked while they were in the car.

"He's doing fine now, yes," Eloise revealed. "Once I started to hum to him he was able to calm down."

"You sing?" Skip asked.

"Oh no," Eloise's face glowed red. "I can only hum. I'm not that good of a singer."

"What do you hum?"

"Just an old tune my grandmother used to sing. I doubt you would know it."

Eloise's house was in sight. "You mentioned wanting to reduce the size of your house. Do you mind if I come in and take a look?"

"I think that would be alright," Eloise responded.

The two of them entered the house, both cats rushed to the door only to run away once Skip was in view. "You have cats?" He asked.

"Yes, Chico and Annie. Annie is always skittish around people. I'm sure Chico will warm up to you soon. Would you like a glass of water?"

"Thank you, Eloise," Skip responded. "If it's not too much trouble."

Skip looked around the living room while Eloise got him some water from the kitchen. Gunsmoke started to play a new episode.

"Do you keep the radio on when you're not home?"

"I keep it on for the cats," Eloise admitted. "And it's nice to come home to the sound of voices."

"Mmh," Skip listened in on the episode.

Eloise came in with his water. "Would you like to listen to the episode?" She offered.

Skip nodded. The two of them ended up sitting on the couch together. They were silent, but they both felt content. Eloise felt as though she was regaining a little bit of what she lost. Skip felt as though he was finally getting something he always needed.

"Poor Chester," Eloise lamented when the show was over.

"Hm? Oh, yes," He agreed. "Poor Chester. For his love to be foiled by Em's younger brother… I can only imagine how he must feel."

Eloise turned to look Skip's way. "It's very late. Do you think you'll be alright driving home?"

"Oh I'll be alright," Skip replied. He stood from the couch and looked around the living room again. "You were right, you have quite a lot of room in this house. It's far too big for just one person."

"I agree," Eloise admitted. "Please let me know if you find a way to help me. However, I would hate to keep you here all night."

"Tomorrow is your day off work, isn't it?" Skip asked.

"Well, yes, it is," Eloise confessed. "But how did you know that?"

"With how often I go to visit my brother I recall never seeing you on Thursdays."

"Oh yes, right," Eloise tucked her curly hair behind her ear. "I would invite you to stay the night but I can only imagine what the neighbors would think, and I hardly believe it's proper with your brother being one of my patients."

"I understand completely, Eloise. I won't be any bother to you."

"Oh, believe me you're no bother, Skip. Thank you for coming tonight."

Skip smiled. "It was a pleasure, miss. I have a lot of work tomorrow but I hope to see you soon."

"I look forward to it," Eloise admitted.

Thursday came and went. Eloise thought about the brothers every moment. When she wasn't worried about how Chase may be doing after such a traumatic encounter, she was battling with her feelings toward Skip. Eloise didn't consider herself very attractive and she could never imagine someone would wish to court her so eagerly, especially now that she was a divorced woman. She wondered if this may be a sign of some good coming into her life. Somehow, later that night, she felt something ominous. It was as though the air around her went cold or that time slowed down for a few seconds. She was just worried about Chase, she convinced herself. She would see him the following day and then she could make sure he's well then.

Yet, as daylight broke through, the ringing of the doorbell alerted Eloise that something was wrong. Still in her gown, she jumped out of bed and hurried to see who was at the front door. She peeked through the peephole and saw a familiar chest with long black strands of hair falling freely above it. She cracked the door open. "Skip? What is it?"

"Eloise." She saw Skip's face, his face glistening. He sniffed and cleared his throat. "Eloise, It's Chase."

Eloise threw on whatever she could find. She wasted no time. Per her request, Skip drove her to work. She couldn't believe what he told her. She couldn't imagine it to be real. She tried several times to wake herself up. This was a dream. This was a joke. This couldn't happen.

The police had already arrived. They investigated every third shift employee. Eloise walked past the interrogations. She walked past the doctors crowding around, talking. She walked despite an officer's call to her to stop where she was. She walked to Chase's door which was wide open and saw just in time as a white sheet covered the young boy's face. She froze.

A policeman gripped her shoulders and turned her around, but she gave him no resistance. Skip retrieved her from the policeman's grasp and hugged her close to him. Eloise made no objection. She saw Chase there, sitting against the wall facing the door, eyes wide but seeing nothing. Mouth open but saying nothing. Face paler than Eloise could imagine possible. He laid there like a rag doll, eyes wide as buttons. It occurred to her that he lived and died in fear. It occurred to her that she would never see Chase ever again. Skip sniffed and hugged Eloise closer. "I overheard the police saying they're looking for my mother. They believe she…" Skip's voice cracked. "They believe she poisoned him."

Eloise's senses felt numb. Sounds were distant, she couldn't see or feel anything, only cry. She couldn't put into words what she saw. She was unable to speak for days after and even then, she never spoke once about that day. She couldn't bring herself to ask who Chase was looking at when he died. Who was there in front of the door?

DEEP SEA MADNESS

Captain Davis spent weeks preparing for his mission. He was certain that he was ready. He saw the submarine for the first time the day he was to begin. "This is the MS-Pebble," His superior informed him.

It had to be as small as possible. Captain Davis knew his objective was to dive into enemy waters and spy on the navy forces to report on the features of their ships and submarines. Captain Davis was to go in alone. The mission was for a week, but Captain Davis packed for two weeks just in case. He wished his friends goodbye.

"Take this with you," His sister insisted. She gave him a small framed photo of their father, the former commander of the navy before he was lost to them by an enemy ship. His body could never be recovered, so Davis and his sister always said that he was watching over them. Every wave that broke on the shore was a sign to them that their father was looking out for them. "He'll give you good luck on your mission," She said.

Captain Davis gave her a nod and a long hug. "You take care of things up here," He told her. "I'll be back before you know it."

Davis entered the Pebble. He listened to the cheers with pride as the Pebble embarked and sank into the depths below. Captain Davis started the long trip towards enemy borders. He listened to coordinates from his superior. He hummed his favorite songs. Captain Davis had been piloting submarines for nearly eight years. He felt at home in the cramped space and the silence. While usually he had a crew, he didn't mind the serenity of a week all on his own. He had the radio to call in his reports and plenty of books for his downtime. He was hardly even nervous about being in enemy waters. He was so small and the little ship was made to be able to dive so deeply that he would be easily overlooked.

Captain Davis had submerged for the crowd, but as he was traveling through friendly waters he remained on the surface. Normal radio signals could reach him that way and Captain Davis enjoyed an occasional word or two with his superior. "There's a lot of water here admiral."

Admiral Smith chuckled. "Get used to it Davis, you're going to be seeing it for seven days."

Enemy waters were fast approaching. Captain Davis called in. "Preparing to dive, Admiral." Once he submerged, he kept himself at 200 meters. He smiled at his father placed by the ELF Radio, his main tool for his mission. Making his way to a depth and location where he was nestled and hidden from enemy ships was easy enough. Captain Davis left the controls and set up his radio to listen in on the enemy's conversations. Once he was set, he grabbed a book and a ham sandwich from his provisions and waited.

There was nothing to report for two days. Captain Davis kept himself busy with reading and sketching in his notepad. With nothing to report, he started journaling as well. 'June 8th, nothing to report. I read most of Moby Dick today. I figured it was about time I gave it a read. I saw a whale this morning. I'm glad it didn't get close.' He looked to the picture of his father. "You're my only company now, dad. You would be so proud to see me walk in your footsteps, I think."

Captain Davis believed day three would be as boring as the rest, but then he heard of something he never heard before. "Has Destiny embarked yet?"

Captain Davis leaned in and fumbled for his pen and notebook.

"Destiny isn't due to embark for another two months. They want her to be perfect."

"Then what was it that embarked yesterday?"

"The test ship, a smaller version of Destiny. What was it called?" There was a pause. "SGB-381. They're running the diving tests and such."

Davis wrote frantically every word he could. Destiny was planning on being able to withstand a test depth of up to 500 meters and hold a total of 200 men. It was unheard of, but here they were, talking about it as though this groundbreaking achievement was just around the corner. It was, in fact, apparently only two months away. What Davis failed to hear, however, was what they planned to do with a sub that went so deep and held so many people? War subs didn't have to go that deep, unless…

'Ping,' Davis sprung out of his chair. 'Ping,' He's been spotted! 'Ping,' They're getting close! Davis rushed to the controls and dove as fast as he could. His report claimed that the enemy submarines had a crush depth of 280 meters at best. The Pebble could go as deep as 350 meters. If Davis could just bottom out and turn off the engine in time, then the submarine pursuing him could lose him. 'Ping,' Davis reached 300 meters. 'Ping,' The enemy sub was still gaining. 'Ping,' Davis moved his sub to a trench nearby and went lower. 'Ping,' 340 Meters, Davis rested The Pebble on the ocean floor and turned off his engine. He held his breath and stood perfectly still.

'Ping... Ping... Ping...' The radar stopped. Davis let his breath out very slowly. He knew instantly the sort of trouble he was in. They knew he was in the trench. Even if they couldn't go down as low, they knew he was there. The Pebble was a one-manned mini-submarine. It had no weapons. It was built to be fast and go deep. The enemy sub, whatever it was, would no doubt have some form of weaponry. It followed Davis past the assumed crush depth with no hesitation. He wondered what other assumptions he made that were wrong.

Davis cautiously started to breathe again. He had to wait out the enemy sub, but for how long? He was stuck in a trench. If they spotted him before he got out, he would have no time to escape enemy fire. Curiously, Davis looked out the small window of the sub. He couldn't see anything. Frustrated, he snuck his way to the picture of his father. He looked down to it. 'Looks like I really got myself in trouble this time, dad,' He thought.

The silence was nearly unbearable. The lack of voices around him left a ringing in his ears. He wondered what his sister was doing just then. Davis sat at the control panel, eyes closed, waiting. He wondered if it was possible to send a distress signal to Admiral Smith, but that thought was quickly snuffed. If it was too dangerous to start the engine and try to get out of the trench then it was certainly too dangerous to try and call for help. Even deep signals wouldn't be able to reach him. He was so close to crush depth that it made him uncomfortable.

Davis' eyes shot open. He looked behind him. Weird, for a moment he thought he heard muttering. He turned to the radio but it was as still as the sub. "Keep it together," He whispered to himself. He was astonished of how much better he felt hearing his own voice.

Day four arrived. Davis slept soundly, but he didn't want to move the submarine yet. It had been less than 24 hours, no doubt the enemy was still waiting for him.

Davis took the opportunity to write in his notes what happened and finish reading Moby Dick. The Sub would occasionally creak, and every time Davis would freeze and wait. He would strain to hear the sonar even though he knew it would sound bright as day. The week came at last. If there was a day to try and escape, Davis thought, this had to be the day. Captain Davis sat at the controls and started the engine. He waited a few seconds. No pings. Davis jolted the sub to life and started to follow the trench a way before ascending his way out of the long, deep crevice.

'Ping ping ping ping," Davis' grip on the wheel nearly failed him. He couldn't believe it, four submarines around him, and they all spotted him in the radar! Quickly, he dove again, deeper, deeper. He watched the dots on his radar getting closer to the trench. He saw them surrounding him. Two more submarines appeared on the screen. As he dove for his life, the lights of The Pebble caught a large gray mass that he was quickly gaining on. "Whale," He cried as he hurried to slow down his sub. Davis was going too fast, he froze and waited for impact.

'Boom,' Davis felt himself jolt violently to the left. 'Crash,' he was knocked violently to the right. 'Thud,' the sub came to a complete halt. The sub's alarm was going off, informing the captain that there was damage. Davis crawled over to the controls and turned off the engine. The pain in his left leg, head and abdomen was indescribable. He was still. He waited to die. He waited for the water to crush him. He waited for a torpedo to hit him. While waiting, he blacked out.

"Harry."

Captain Davis' eyes shot open. He didn't know what was worse, the ringing in his ears or the pounding in his head. Davis groaned and rolled over, clutching his stomach. "Ow," He shouted when the pain in his leg shot up his entire body. 'Ping,' the radar went and Davis instantly froze. Was he still in the Pebble? Were they still looking for him? This was no good, maybe they were waiting for him to try and escape again.

"Harry."

Davis' eyes shot over to the picture of his father. The picture was laying at arm's reach, glass shattered on the frame. "Dad?" He whispered. Davis dragged himself to the wall and propped himself into a sitting position. His head was spinning, his side was bruised, and he was sure that his leg was broken. He scanned the sub which had little to no light. All he could see was the sharp red blinking on the console and the portrait Davis had in his hands. The voice he was hearing before was undoubtedly his father's voice. The sound of his father calling him by his first name was such a clear memory that Davis was sure he was suffering a concussion which caused him to hear it. Even so, it made his heart ache for home.

"Dad," He muttered. "I think I'm going to die here." Davis took stock of the situation. He had a month of water but only a week of food. He was in need of medical assistance and he was no doubt past the Pebble's crushing point. He was either going to get sick and die, starve and die, get crushed by the ocean and die, or get torpedoed and die. His eyes watered from the pain and the hopelessness of his situation. He was scared. He was alone. The only witnesses to his existence now were the unknown and unforgiving creatures that swam 260 fathoms deep. Davis quieted his ragged breaths and cradled his stomach while resting against the wall. The pain and the dizziness were too much. He fell asleep once more.

"Harry, don't lose hope."

Davis opened his eyes softly, the red light blinking, a tall figure stood before him. Davis was too tired to respond.

"What is this? Are you just going to quit and let yourself die? I thought I raised you better than that."

"Dad?" Davis whispered. "You're dead," He stated.

"And you're not yet," The shadow figure replied. "If you just sit here you're going to be like me before long."

Davis' head rested against the wall. "I'm in so much pain. Maybe it's better if I die."

"Harry your nation and your sister need you. You can't let go now."

Davis was silent for a moment. He turned his head and spotted the water supply and the cooler with a sandwich waiting for him. His stomach growled.

"Focus on the goal and go for it, Harry. Keep your eyes on the goal."

Davis dragged himself across the room to the water supply. His leg had gone numb. If he didn't look back or feel the resistance in his dragging, he would have thought the leg was gone. Davis gripped the faucet. He grabbed a cup that fell on the floor during the crash. The moment the water reached his lips, Davis felt as though he was regaining his own life. He pulled open the cooler and grabbed a sandwich. He unwrapped the clear plastic and stuffed nearly half of the sandwich in his mouth in one bite.

Remembering his father, he turned back to the figure only to see the red blinking light catching nothing except the shadows that were always there. "Dad?" He called out to no avail. Davis put a hand to his head. It was the concussion, that's all it was.

He felt his chest tighten.

After he had some food, Davis looked around for cloth and support for his leg. He wrapped it up in old bandages and blankets in an attempt to keep his leg still when he moved around. Davis barely succeeded but it was better than nothing. "Okay," He said to himself. "Time to assess the situation." Davis first checked to see how deep he was. 480 meters. He felt a lump form in his throat. He wanted to see if the engine would run, but he couldn't make enough noise that the radars of the other submarines could find him. Davis looked out the window.

Everything was completely dark. The vast black depths were like a brick wall in front of him. Davis wondered if he was, in fact, facing a wall until he saw in the distance some sort of light. Davis strained to look harder. At first, he thought it could be a school of bioluminescent fish, but if they were, they would be strangely stationary in their swimming pattern. Davis' eyes widened. Was it a submarine? If it was, it would be huge. Bigger than any submarine he's ever seen. He thought again about Destiny. "How long have I been out?" He felt a chill up his spine.

He remembered that the soldiers were talking about how Destiny wasn't due to see water for two months. Could it be one of the prototypes? No, it was too big. It was the size of a ship.

It was a ship.

How could there be a ship this deep? In fact, Davis realized that the more he looked at it, the more he could see the outline. The lights in the windows were bright, warm and comforting. The sails were tattered but otherwise it looked pristine in shape. It occurred to him that he was seeing the ship better and better because it was moving closer and closer.

'Ping,' Davis' bones chilled to stillness.

'Ping,' The signal was the ship.

'Ping,' It was getting closer.

Could the other subs pick it up out of the trench? Why was a large ship signaling the sonar, and how did it dive into such a dangerous depth? Unless…

Davis shook his head and closed his eyes. He waited until the sound of the sonar died out. With a sigh, he opened his eyes.

Revisiting the window, Davis reeled back and nearly fell over on his leg again. What was looking back at him was a round, white sphere with odd, smaller lights blinking and watching him. Captain Davis stood perfectly still, besides the trembling. He held his breath save for the short bursts that escaped from genuine trepidation. Davis was petrified, staring down the bizarre thing that kept its gaze so intensely before sinking down and away. Davis rushed to the window to see where the thing went. Below him, the sea floor shifted and turned and slithered its way down the trench.

"I have to write this down," Davis realized.

He wrote down everything that happened from the escape attempt to the strange eye looking at him and the mysterious underwater ghost ship.

"Do you think anyone will believe you if they ever read the journal?" The captain's father asked from behind him.

Davis spun around to see, of course, no one. "Of course. I have no doubt they would read it. I was sent here as a spy, no one is more capable than myself. Of course, the journal will be nothing if we end up getting crushed by the ocean." Davis froze. "I meant to say if I get crushed," He corrected.

Days more passed by. It was hard for Davis to keep track. He wasn't able to rest as well as he hoped with a leg being broken. The pain woke him up often. However, there were some moments of complete silence where he was able to sleep despite the pain.

'Ping,' Davis' eyes shot open. 'Ping,' He got up as fast as he could see what the sonar was picking up. 'Ping,' He looked out the window and saw, once more, the ship passing through the trench. He felt a pit in his stomach drop. He tried to gather as much information as he could about the ship. He looked around for the creature. He searched for the giant glowing eyes as big as the Pebble. He scribbled the details of the ship, doodling as fast as he could. The ship faded away, and in its place, there was the brick-thick blackness. Immediately following that blackness, however, there was the orb of lights staring into the window with such desire and curiosity. "It's just an illusion," Davis' shaky voice began. "Davis, there are no underwater ships. There are no large bright-eyed monsters. There is no ghost of your father."

"Are you sure about that?" He heard a voice ask. He turned to the picture of his father that he since propped against the control console. "Yes, I'm perfectly sure. All of this isn't real. None if it can be real." The eye faded away like it did before and Davis was left alone with his father.

"You know you have to get out of here son," Davis said.

"I know dad," Harry replied. "I've run out of food. I think, maybe, it's time to assess the situation." Harry started to limp as he paced, leaning against desk and chairs and the control console when he could. "Every few days, the ship arrives and my radar goes off. Maybe the enemy's radar goes off for the ship as well. The monster comes around at the same time."

Davis pivoted and kept limping. "I thought you said you didn't believe they existed."

Harry pivoted and kept limping. "I did, but maybe, the other subs can see it too."

"Do you think you can sneak out while the enemy is distracted from the ship?" Davis asked.

"It's the only chance I have to survive. If I stay here much longer, I'll surely go mad," Harry concluded. "Okay. So the next time the ship arrives I'll start the engine and go the opposite direction as fast as the sub can go." With his plan made and his mind set, he went to lie down and see if he could manage just a few more hours of sleep.

Three days without food. These days were easy to record because Davis' stomach refused to let him forget. In almost as many days he was unable to sleep. Davis kept his attention to the window. He waited for the ship.

"Remember, your nation and your sister are counting on you to tell them about Destiny," Davis said.

"I know, dad," Harry responded.

"If you make it out of here alive," Davis told himself. "Just know that I'm very proud of you."

Harry quickly turned his head the other direction. "Do you mean it, dad?"

"I do," Davis turned his head again. He nodded. "You did good, son."

'Ping,' Captain Davis stood up. 'Ping,' He fumbled to the controls and resurrected the Pebble's engine. 'Ping,' Davis ignored the loud flashing warning signs. He ignored the other subs that appeared on the radar. There were four, six, eight, nine subs total. Davis trusted the subs to be confused between his and the underwater ship's signals. Four ships were going after him. Davis went faster, the adrenaline and liberation causing his hands to tremble. He started to laugh through his nose softly, then louder and more confident as the Pebble sped away and left the enemy subs behind.

He was free.

"Yes! Yes, I did it," He screamed and cheered. The sub's tank was leaking. He was running low on fuel, air and speed. Captain Davis prepared to breach the ocean surface. Once the sub found its way to open air, the Pebble's engine gave out. Davis was able to shoot two flares up into the sky. There was no power, no radio signal, and no food, but Davis was in friendly waters again. He had no doubt that help was on the way. He wrote the details of his daring escape in the journal, unaware of the large dark shadow that began to rise below him.

Once the rescue team arrived hours later, they were greeted with the sight of a floating, open submarine named the MS-Pebble. A detail of three marines and two medics searched the cramped submarine for clues. They found the flare gun that was shot two hours before. They found a bundle of blankets and bandages and they found the journal. However, the captain that embarked on the mission with the Pebble was nowhere to be found. Once his sister received the news, she was devastated. She demanded to read the journal he left behind, but Admiral Smith strongly recommended against it. She would not be satisfied, however, and Smith reluctantly let her read it.

The details of Destiny were taken into account, and with the warning a month in advance it changed the tide of the war. The rest of the entries, however, the captain's sister was able to keep as his next of kin. She thought of burning it and along with it all the evidence of her brother being driven mad. However, one detail terrified her to the core and instead of kindling turned the journal of madness into an heirloom. The coordinates Davis wrote where he breached, the location where the last traces of him remained, were the same coordinates of the ship their father was in before his body was lost to the sea.

EMPTY EYES

June tapped a nail into her wall. She wasn't sure if just one nail would do it, but she hoped that it wouldn't at least end in disaster. She hit the nail so that it was almost all the way in. Satisfied, she raised the painting in position. After a little bit of adjusting, she took a step back to review her work. "There," She gleamed.

The dead-eyed child looked back at June, observing her. June looked back at the girl in the painting. "You like it, too don't you? I can tell. Much better than that drafty old attic, anyway."

June thought that her mother got rid of the painting decades ago, but when she and her older brother were packing up their mother's things June was surprised to see a lot of old precious memories in the attic. Her smile melted a little bit thinking of her mother. The funeral was two weeks ago. June and her brother Cecil sold their childhood home and split the profit. It was a hard and heartbreaking decision. Looking to the painting, she was relieved to have a little bit of the house left over.

"It's a shame that it was something like this that brought us together after so long, huh?" Cecil asked while the siblings had lunch together.

"I can't believe the house sold so quickly," June whispered, holding onto her lemonade with both hands. "What are we going to do with the rest of mom's stuff?"

Cecil heaved a heavy sigh. "Sell it, maybe. It'll help pay off a little of the funeral. We could have a yard sale, you know, like the ones mom took us to every summer when we were kids."

June smiled briefly. "Oh yeah, she would give us twenty dollars each and we would drive around to the yard sales around town, looking for stuff worth our little allowance. You started your baseball card collection that way."

"That's also how our house became like a hoarding nest," Cecil laughed. He took a sip of his soda. The two of them were silent for a while, communicating through shared nostalgia. June felt her eyes water. "I miss her," She choked.

"Yeah," Cecil fought back his own grief. "I see you kept the creepy painting," He gestured to her living room wall, trying to keep the conversation light.

Thankful for a distraction, June argued. "It's not creepy. I remember mom kept that painting for a few years. It was always in the living room."

"You remember why mom put it up in the attic, don't you?"

"No," June raised an eyebrow. "Why?"

"You started to say to her that the girl in the picture was your best friend. You would wander around talking about how you and 'Lucy' were going to do various awful things. You and I had a pretty big fight and you told mom you and Lucy were going to 'make me bleed' and she hid the painting up in the attic from you."

"What? No, you're making that up. I don't remember any of that at all."

"I'm telling you, it's what happened."

"I think you're lying." Even though June felt confident that Cecil was just trying to scare her, she started to feel the back of her neck burn, as though someone was staring at her with an intensity.

That night, she went to bed early so she could help Cecil with the yard sale the next day. It wasn't long after everything went dark and silent that she stirred from her sleep. Someone turned the hallway light on. She turned to face her bedroom door when, just at the doorway, she saw a little girl. The girl stood there, eyes black as tar, sucking her in. The little girl opened her mouth and it hung there a moment until June heard a small echoing, but familiar voice.

"I missed you, June. Let's go play."

June shot up into bed. Just as quickly she heard a 'click' as the light turned back off and the image of the little girl no longer stood at the doorway. She stared at the doorway, waiting for her heart rate to go down. As soon as she gathered the courage, she closed the door and went back to sleep.

The click of the light came on again. The little girl stood at the doorway. Her head tilted unnaturally to one side. "We can play forever now, June."

"Stop!" It took a lot of energy to force the scream out of June's throat. Her body was so heavy. She was finding it harder and harder to keep her eyes open. She wanted to get up and run out of the house, but she was just so tired. The light turned off again.

When the light turned on for the last time, the little girl stood beside the bed, her hungry eyes fixed on June. June did her best not to look, trying to will away the vision. This was only a dream, a terror. This wasn't real. It couldn't be real. Cold fingers began to tickle at her neck. It was getting harder and harder to breathe. She could hear the little girl's echoing giggle. "Let's play forever."

The following morning, June and Cecil started a yard sale for all of their mother's old things. Among these things, there was a picture of a young girl, eyes large and soulful, leaning against a box of old tapes with a 99 cent sticker on the frame. They watched as a young man came and bought the painting. Cecil watched his sister wave it goodbye. "June, I thought you were fond of that painting. Are you sure you want to get rid of it?"

June turned to look at Cecil, her smile weak, eyes tired and sunken, almost empty. There was a faint curl up of her lips. "I'm sure."

IN LOO OF CONVERSATION

Kevin had a rough Sophomore year. The person he liked turned out to be in love with someone else, his father lost his job, he wasn't able to help their football team win a single game in the season, and worst of all, his mother passed away. She went out one night and then never came back. Her body was found near the edge of a cliff. It was a complete mystery what happened, and the case got cold. While everyone else seemed to go on with life, Kevin couldn't let it go. He didn't cry out or break down in front of anyone. He wouldn't talk about it, he remained in the moment where he found out his mother was gone. He saw her just the night before. She said goodnight to him. Ever since, Kevin was distant, in a sort of emotional constipation.

There was an old school rumor that if someone sat on the toilet in the darkness, they could be granted a dark wish by saying 'We need to talk,' three times and then saying what you wished for. The catch was, the wish would be granted in a horrible way, much like the tale of the Monkey's Paw. Only the most desperate people would think of summoning the dark wish. Kevin was certainly desperate enough.

He sat on the toilet lid with the lights off. He had to be honest, he felt nervous only doing this much. Kevin let in a deep breath, then slowly let it out. The sooner he did it, the sooner he could leave. He wasn't too sure if stupid school rumors would hold any truth, but it was for his mother. "Okay. We need to talk, we need to talk, we need to talk." He sat there, silent. He didn't hear anything strange or bizarre. He didn't feel any different, either. Maybe he did it wrong, or it was just a stupid rumor after all. Regardless, he made his wish. After all, you never knew. "I wish I could see the dead."

After another couple of seconds of silence, Kevin gave up. He turned on the light and left the bathroom. Kevin felt the last of his hopes drain from him. He hoped to be able to ask his mother what happened to her. Most believed that she just fell off the cliff. Kevin was the only one who thought that something didn't make sense. His mother never went out on her own, especially somewhere as secluded as the woods. Kevin went back into his room and cradled his head with his hands. He knew he'd likely be driven mad without closure.

"If I could just have a chance to talk to my mother," Kevin thought out loud. "Then maybe-," But his words were cut short. Out the corner of his eye, he thought he saw her head towards the living room. Kevin rushed out of his room to the living room to make sure.

"Kevin, where are you going?" His father called out from the couch.

"I won't be out long," Kevin called back.

"It's dark outside Kevin, at least grab-,"

"I'm fine dad, I promise! I'll be right back, just…" He watched as the faint vision of his mother phased through the front door. "Just going out for a bit of fresh air." Kevin followed her. He followed her around the block. He followed her towards the train tracks. He followed her out of town.

Night was coming quickly. Kevin couldn't see much of anything. He wished that he remembered to bring his phone or if he took the flashlight with him, but he couldn't lose sight of his mother. Her glowing form was his only light as he pressed on through the tall grass. Kevin thought about going back, but even if she were a ghastly phantom, Kevin trusted his mother to guide him in the right direction. He wished that she could slow down a little bit.

"Mom, where are we going," He called out to her. She didn't respond. His legs were starting to get tired. "Mom, please slow down, I need to take a break." There was still no response.

Kevin followed even as the bushes he walked through scratched at his legs. Kevin followed even as the darkness hid everything from sight except for the sight of his mother. The bushes became forest. He recognized this path. It was near where they found his mother's body. "Mom," He wheezed. "Please just tell me where…"

The ground gave up beneath him. Kevin fell so suddenly that he didn't have time to scream. He didn't have time to scold himself for forgetting about the cliff they saw his mother near. He had no time for anything, it was just the sound of a crack, the sensation of falling, pain, then blackness.

Kevin's eyes shot open. He looked around to see that he was surrounded by trees and bushes. He sat up and rubbed his eyes. 'Where's mom,' He thought before turning to look behind him.

Two large white bulging orbs looked right back at him. Kevin jumped back, too terrified to make a sound. He saw a corpse hanging from the vines. One vine cut into the corpse's neck, the rest of it suspended midair by the vines surrounding it. Kevin recognized the corpse right away. He tried to scream, but he could make no sound. He tried to pull the body down from the vines, but his hands couldn't connect with them. He looked at himself in sheer terror, dangling from the cliff. He fell to his knees, paralyzed at the sight of his mangled body.

Farther away into the mist, there was a white light. It was the whitest anything he'd ever seen. The mist swirled about, the image enticing and warm. Even so, the desire to find out what happened to his mother was too strong. 'I can't die yet,' he thought. 'I can't die until I find out what happened. It can't be this sudden. I don't have any answers yet!' The light faded and Kevin took a few steps back from his body. His desperate curiosity kept him in place, and then the curiosity consumed him. He didn't think he'd ever felt an emotion this strong before. 'Why' was the only word that would cycle through his being. Why? Everything felt like a dream. He was rapidly forgetting what being alive felt like. All he could feel was 'Why?' Until soon, he felt something else.

He felt like he was being watched.

Reluctantly, Kevin turned his attention to the woods behind him. There, he could see them. There were men, women, children, animals, all facing him with their emotionless, blank-eyed expressions. Kevin saw that with the rest of the crowd, there was his mother. Uncaring, staring, unflinching. Kevin could feel the last of himself waft away as though it were the remnants of a dream. The mental picture of his family, friends and life materialized in the cold eyes of the beings that faded before him. Any logical thinking was replaced with 'Why?' Soon, the image of the trees and bushes and even his dead body faded until all he could see were ghosts.

HIDE

Hide. Just hide. Danger is everywhere. Something is coming.

These were not words, but feelings. It cowers within itself. Even though the places around it would change, it continues to hide. It continues to cower. Something is coming. It doesn't know what the Something is or what will happen once the Something came, but It knew to hide. It made itself small. It hid in darkness and in shadows and just within the field of vision. It made no sound nor did it have a defining characteristic or form. It didn't know what it was, it just needed to hide.

Just hide. Nothing else mattered. Don't stay in the same place for long or the Something would find it for sure. It hid in radio signals. It hid in black and white televisions. It hid in the whispering wind at the dead of night.

Danger was everywhere. The Something had spies and eyes and ears and knew where It hid. It hid from the eyes of cats and other creatures which followed it, watched it, analyzed it. It trembled at the sound of a rooster's crow and only felt solace in the still, dark silence. It shielded itself away from sudden movements and loud noises and bright lights. It did not know what it was, only that It existed and It wanted to survive. The way to survive was to hide.

Something was coming. It was losing speed. Something was gaining. It was desperate to rest. Something was pursuing it. It was getting so tired. Something extended sharp claws and bared sharp teeth and excreted a low, guttural growl from its wavering existence. It hid in the form of a small doll with button eyes and a stitched-on smile. Something was waiting, so It found protection in the doll. It sewed its being to the burlap doll and fell dormant. It was safe. It rested. Sleep, rest, relax. It waited. It waited for someone to come. It waited for someone to come for the doll; a dormant little trinket.

SWEAT

Kyu-Yeon was a logger. He was hired to travel to many large forests and take down mass amounts of trees for various productions. Recently he was sent to a project with a group smaller than usual. He wasn't sure that he would be comfortable with this project, but he was lucky enough to have his closest friend Sun-Wang with him. He was spending his lunch break with Sun-Wang when he said, "I'm surprised they had us work in this forest. I can't imagine the natives will be happy."

Kyu-Yeon chuckled, "Since when does Corporate care what other people think?"

His friend shook his head. "Well if any of the stories I heard about this forest are true, they should start listening for once."

Kyu-Yeon turned his body towards him, setting down his sandwich. "What kind of stories have you heard?"

"This forest is enchanted, I hear," Sun-Wang explained. "Strange creatures, a path to the spirit realm, and most disturbing of all, a demon that sweats blood."

"I think I lost my appetite," Kyu-Yeon muttered as he pushed away his food.

"You asked me to tell you," His friend reminded him. "The natives were shouting at me earlier, telling me 'Tuhinga Kuini, Tuhinga Kuini, she'll get you she'll come to you tonight.'"

"I'm pretty sure we're not allowed to talk to the natives."

"Their stories are interesting."

"We're enemies destroying their land. Getting to know them is just going to make it harder to do your job," Kyu-Yeon warned.

"They know we're just workers for the real assholes up in corporate. It wasn't our idea to work here. I think they know that. They've been trying to convince me to quit."

"See?" Kyu-Yeon replied. "But if you quit your job you can't send money to your family. You can't eat, you can't afford your house, they could just be lying to you about these stories."

"I don't know," Sun-Wang muttered. "They seem pretty serious about this forest. It was fine when it was land corporate bought but this job is illegal. They're just hoping that no one catches on until we give them as much wood as possible. They know that most people don't care about the natives. It's kind of awful."

"Sun-Wang, I get your concern, I'm worried too. But we're just the workers. The best thing we can do is hope that people catch on soon and we get sent to do work that's legal after the corporation faces backlash."

"But the natives suffer in the meantime," Sun-Wang sighed. "I don't know, maybe I will quit. I was thinking of protesting but... No one else is willing to protest with me."

"Take a sick day, maybe," Kyu-Yeon suggested. "Give yourself some time to think about this. A lot is at stake for you if you quit. It's harder than ever for immigrants to find work these days."

After lunch, Sun-Wang called in sick. Kyu-Yeon was right, he needed some time to think. Later that night, Kyu-Yeon stumbled into his temporary hut, mind reeling and exhausted from a long day's work. He peeled off his sweat-drenched clothes and hurried to the shower for relief. As he was drying, he heard a loud buzzing in his right ear. He cried out and rapidly waved his hand near his head. He scanned the room for the culprit. There, resting on the wall was a little mosquito. "Eugh!" He exclaimed as he whacked the wall with his towel. Confident that he got it, he finished getting dressed for bed. His right arm itched and he felt a bump in his skin. "Fucker got me," He muttered. Well, at least it was just the one.

Kyu-Yeon walked into his bedroom, scratching at the bite when he heard buzzing again. He halted, eyes peering through every inch of the room when he noticed three more mosquitoes flying around. "This time, I'll be thorough," He promised the room as he picked up a sandal and went on his hunt. One after another, the three mosquitoes went down, but even as he did he found five more flying around. "This is ridiculous," Kyu-Yeon growled. He grabbed a can of bug spray from under the sink and headed back to his room.

When he opened the door again, his eyes went wide. He lost the ability to speak. The room, once empty save for a few pests, now had a swarm so large the room was nearly black. Before Kyu-Yeon could decide whether to spray at the swarm or flee, he was surrounded by the darkness. He pushed the spray can on, screaming, waving it wildly, trying to escape. He couldn't see. He couldn't think, and soon he couldn't even breathe. Moments of agony went by. The can went empty but he still pressed the button. Against one he was able to squash it easily, but a swarm, no matter how big he was, was too much for him to handle.

The next morning the logging corporation was distraught to hear that every employee they sent to log in the forest of the natives had either died or went missing. They were forced to retreat from the project and the story of the mysterious deaths became mainstream conversation. Millions heard the scandal of the illegal logging work and how everyone sent there except for one died or mysteriously disappeared. Many people believed it was the natives, but Sun-Wang would say to anyone that would listen how his best friend and former coworkers were eaten alive by Tuhinga Kuini for trying to destroy her sacred forest.

DEMON ALPHABET: A HELPFUL GUIDE

A is for Astral, the plane where they thrive
B is for Bestial that live to survive
C is for Cryptids, don't answer their call
D is for Devils, most famous of all
E is for Eaters, consumers of fun
F is for Fae, the mischievous ones
G is for Gods and the deities of old
H is for Hunger, they feast on your soul
I is for friends of the Imaginary skill
J is for Jinn said to have free will
K is for kfor which most tend to trust
L is for Lickers who tend to disgust
M is for Mind, they all are born here
N is for Nightmare, they feed off of fear
O is for Omen both evil and kind
P for Personal, prevent your unwind
Q is for Questions and all left unanswered
R is for Reiki, a good thing to master
S is for Shadows, possessor of beings
T is for Trinkets, possessor of things
U is for Universe, Feel them in you
V is for Villain, or is Victim more true?
W is for Wights, demons of season
X is for Xhinde, they slam doors for no reason
Y is for Youkai, one of their many names
Z is for Zozo, do not play his games.

I GOT AWAY WITH IT

Your mind does the strangest things in order to cope with you doing something horrible. No matter what it is, if you have any shred of conscience, you spend a period of time replaying the moment over and over again. You try to tell yourself it was a dream or you try to erase it from your mind completely. Even though the deed has already been done, you have a moment of illusion where you think that something can be done about it, but you can't.

Over time, however, people forget. Life goes on and it is crazy and always keeping you busy. You find yourself not even thinking about what you'd done, and every time you rediscover the memory the tragedy of it fades little by little. It may even feel like at some point it happened to someone else, like a story you heard before.

Other days on occasion you will find yourself letting your guilt consume you. For me, the guilt manifests itself like a woman sitting on my chest, her face twisted into a scream, staring at me with eyes that beg 'why?'

But is there normally a reason? I know that, for me, it was spur of the moment. I wasn't really thinking, or whatever thoughts I did have seem stupid now. It also seems to always involve an outside source. People always want a simple explanation, but explanations are never really so simple, are they? Meanwhile I go about my life, usually sleeping just fine, forgetting what happened like a bad movie. Yet sometimes the woman rests on my chest, her face getting closer and closer.

Your mind will sometimes alter the memory to make it not seem so bad. What exactly happened blurs from time to time, but the outcome is always the same. No one caught me. I will tell myself a lot how one day I won't remember at all, but what justice then gets served? When everyone forgets, who will be left to remember?

Then I remember her. Her eyes stare at me, unblinking. The weight on my chest made it hard to breathe. She will remember. She will make sure I never fully forget. It is even possible, should she decide to, her gaping mouth might one day swallow me whole.

RORY

Rory hated his job. His alarm radio woke him at five almost every day. He had one hour to get to work almost every day. He got dressed and ready, able to get to the asylum and clock in about three minutes early almost every day. He brushed his bright red hair out of his brown eyes and stretched out his back, finding pleasure in every 'pop' it made. He went to wake up the patients.

There were a few core rules that every employee had to abide by. One was to never leave a patient unattended unless they were in their room. The second was that if a caretaker ever felt themselves losing their patience, they had to call someone to relieve them and settle down. This prevented caretakers from taking it out on the patients, many of whom had been abused a great deal before. The third and most annoying rule, according to Rory, that if a patient is hallucinating or being delusional, the caretaker is to not try to disprove it but to keep them calm and comfortable, even if it meant humoring their whims and playing along.

It was this rule alone that caused Rory to despise his job. Some patients were alright, but he didn't understand why everyone had to 'humor' them. He didn't believe that going along with their fantasies was helping at all. He wanted to cure these people. He didn't want to just pretend with them while he watched them waste away. Before he completely hated his job, he cared for an older woman named Francine who passed away months ago. Rory could talk with her. She always wanted to know what was going on. She wasn't scared of the truth.

Like all workers, Rory dealt with many, if not all of the patients. Although while the majority of patients could do many mundane tasks on their own, there was one customer in the increased care district that Rory was solely responsible for during his shift.

"Wakey wakey Chase, time to start the day!" Rory chimed as he turned on the light and walked into the padded room. There Chase Finney lay in his bed; a sixteen-year-old boy diagnosed with a heavy case of schizophrenia.

The boy sat up in bed so quickly it seemed to make him a little dizzy. He darted his head left and right, searching for something. "Where are they?" Chase asked.

"There is no 'they,' Chase. Just you and me," Rory sighed. The kid's imaginary creatures were usually the most difficult thing about getting him to do anything. No matter how many times Rory told him there was no such thing as demons or monsters.

"Go away. I don't want you here!" The kid exclaimed, shielding himself with his arms.

Almighty the kid was annoying, but whatever was wrong with his head, Rory at least knew how to handle it... Most of the time. "Come on big baby, we have to eat breakfast and shower and change your clothes. We're having eggs, sausage and pancakes today. All your favorites."

Chase brought down his defenses. Good, that got him. "Can-can... I... Have coffee? Wh-... With my... Um... Meal?"

Coffee seemed to calm Chase down best. It didn't seem healthy for a boy his age but hey, whatever worked. Rory shrugged, "Sure, why not? Come on. You have to hold my hand, remember?"

Chase whimpered and set his feet on the floor, quickly retracted, then committed the second time. He shuffled his feet along the side of his wall, looking down at an invisible obstacle. Rory presented his hand and watched in mild amusement as Chase did a little hop and stumble before taking a frantic grasp of Rory's hand. The caretaker steadied him. "You made it, good job," he held back a bittersweet chuckle. Jeez, it just felt like he was making fun of the guy.

Rory took Chase with him to the cafeteria. There were several patients there, each one with their primary day caretakers. For caretakers that didn't have someone they looked after in the advanced care unit, they would have several patients. One patient was throwing a fit in the corner, but the others were eating relatively peacefully. Rory tried to let go of Chase's hand but the kid had an iron grip on him. Rory sighed and took Chase to the cafeteria ladies. The kid's eyes and head darted around occasionally but he was still following Rory with no complaints so the caretaker cared little about it.

As he took the boy to a table to sit, Chase stopped walking behind him. Rory felt the tug of his hand and turned to look back and saw Chase staring in terror out the window. He followed his gaze towards the window and saw nothing there. He sighed. "Chase, just ignore it. Come on, we have to get you to eat."

"But," Chase muttered.

Rory squeezed Chase's hand which seemed to bring him back

to what little sense he had. 'Poor kid,' Rory thought. He wished that he could just tell Chase that he was hallucinating. He wanted desperately to let the kid know that all the danger was fake and that he was safe. He always tried, but it was as if he never heard him. The caretaker hid Chase's morning medicine in his food and watched the kid eat. When Chase was eating it was normally the calmest Rory ever got to see him. He took a closer look at the kid. Besides the ghostly pale face and deep bags under his eyes, Chase looked like any normal child. Rory realized how scarily easy it was to disassociate the patients from human beings. He never remembered having that distant feeling towards Francine before she passed away.

Chase sipped his coffee with a grin. "My Wiggy, this coffee is magnificent."

"Mm hmm," Rory offered.

"I simply must know where you get your beans, dear boy."

"Dippin' Doughnuts," Rory replied.

"Cambodia you say, how delightful!"

Rory rubbed his eyes.

When his shift was over, Rory wasted no time to get home. He saw Eloise briefly. He didn't know how she ever got the job. As far as he was concerned, she was too sensitive for work like theirs. Rory was courteous to her, but spoke as little as possible. She was more than a working woman. The whole city knew about her divorce. Her husband was a doctor and he was considered to be something like a genius. Rory didn't know much about Eloise, but for someone like that to leave her there had to be a reason.

Rory's wife, however, was the most perfect woman in his opinion. He couldn't wait to come home and see her and his son Junior. Because of that, the sight of Eloise was a welcome one. Rory drove home listening to the radio. He was fond of the music, but he and his wife would always tune in to listen to their favorite radio show, Gunsmoke. There was a new episode coming on the following day.

Rory came home to the television playing and his lovely wife doing the dishes. "Afternoon honey," Rory gave her a kiss on the cheek.

"How was work today, dear?" She asked him.

"It was the same as any other day," Rory replied. "Where's Junior?"

"He's upstairs playing with his friend Bo."

"Oh alright," Rory conceded. He hugged his wife from behind. He gave her another kiss. "How was your day?"

"Oh," She sighed, leaning into him. "Busy, but nothing worth talking about."

These were the moments Rory loved; being with his wife, having dinner with his family, being around sane people. He remembered when he was young and naïve and thought that he would be making a difference coming to work at the asylum. Now he understood that all the caretakers at the asylum were only better paid babysitters for people that weren't all there. They were just waiting for each patient to die.

After supper, Rory slept soundly in the bed he shared with his wife. When he woke up, he went through his routine, like every day. "I'll see you tonight," He kissed his wife goodbye. Rory woke up his other patients before going to Chase. "Good morning kid, time for breakfast."

Chase jolted awake and started to cry out right away. "Gaining, they're gaining! B-broken door, hide, hide in the bathroom!"

"Chase, buddy it's just me," Rory called out.

The boy's eyes darted around wildly as he pressed himself to the wall before his eyes fell onto Rory. "Wiggy, ol' bean, what are you doing in a place like this?"

"It's breakfast time, Chase," Rory sighed. He held out his hand and waited for the patient to make his way to him. "Hurry up before it gets cold. If you want, you can even have some more of that coffee you like so much."

"O-oh," Chase climbed down from his bed and took careful steps to Rory until he was able to take the hand offered to him. "That sounds delightful Wiggy, thank you."

"Yeah, don't mention it," Rory muttered.

Rory worked the day on autopilot. He was thinking about spending time with his wife and his son. He was thinking about hearing the next new episode of Gunsmoke, the only real reason he still had a radio in his house. He didn't prepare himself for the visit of his least favorite person in the world.

"Doctor Figg, Mrs. Finney is here to see her son."

"Aw shit," He muttered. "Alright, I'll bring Chase to the visiting room." Rory turned to Chase who was lost in his own tea parties. "Chase," He called to him.

"Yes, Wiggy?"

"There is someone here to meet you."

Chase's smile faded a little, but Rory was able to get him to the visiting room. The patient sat first on one end of the table with the caretaker beside them, while the visitor was ushered in afterwards. Chase would routinely have four visitors. Occasionally, his aunt would arrive who he adored. She played along with him in his hallucinations and he always called her Maggie, although her name was Grace. Chase also enjoyed seeing his brother who visited nearly half of the week. Rory rarely saw him since he came in only when Eloise was working. Rory liked to see Chase's father, Mr. Finney, but he only came to visit his son on his birthday and the kid never spoke around him. The final visitor who always came in the mornings and far too often was the mother, Mrs. Finney. Chase hated her, and so did Rory. Neither of them would enjoy her visiting. Rory went so far as to see what he could do to make her unfit as a visitor, but the Head of Department claimed that she never showed any intention to harm the patient so she was still allowed to come as she pleased. Besides, Chase benefitted from going through routine and she was a constant.

It was close to the end of Rory's shift. He supposed he could stand her for fifteen minutes before leaving it for Eloise to do. If Eloise was as fond of Chase as she said, Rory was sure she wouldn't mind.

Another caretaker sent Mrs. Finney in. Chase's body tensed. Rory could feel his breathing quicken. "Good afternoon, Mrs. Finney," He offered halfheartedly.

"Good afternoon Dr. Figg. Hello Chase," She turned to her son and gave him a smile that Rory could only imagine was meant to be sweet and reassuring. "Can you hear me?" She asked him.

'He's in the same room with you, of course he can,' Rory thinks. He doesn't respond, however. She came to visit her son and Rory would do no favors in arguing with her. He was there just as a guide. He was there to make sure that no fight broke out, so he always did what he could to speak as little as possible. That was always hardest to do with Mrs. Finney. All her questions were always directed towards the caretaker.

"Does he still see the demons?" She asked Rory.

"He still hallucinates, yes," Rory muttered. "Why don't you ask Chase about it?"

She ignored his comment. "Does he visit with the priest?"

"There is a priest on call that comes to give prayer to patients who request it, but again, you should ask Chase. I'm only here half the time, I don't know if he calls on the priest."

"He wouldn't call the priest on his own," Mrs. Finney concluded. "Devils are within him, don't you see?"

Rory saw Chase clutch his chair harder.

"Mrs. Finney with all due respect, Chase's condition is purely a scientific case. He takes medicine and he is better than he was when he arrived."

"The demons have you fooled," Mrs. Finney glared. "My boy is being possessed by horrible creatures and your medicine is only prolonging their effect. Do you honestly believe that you can make the people here better by throwing pills into their mouths?"

"Occupancy has dropped since these medicines were used by a drastic amount," Rory informed her. He was starting to raise his voice. Those who discredited science like Mrs. Finney irritated him more than anyone, but he would be foolish to not also be aware that the medicine wasn't helping everyone. Although he believed more medicine would be invented with time to help more people, people like Mrs. Finney used every excuse to believe that everything was the work of some unexplained mysterious entity. Worse of all, every time she talked about this stuff in front of Chase, it always made him relapse into an episode that could sometimes take the rest of the day to calm him down from.

"I'm surprised at you Mr. Figg. I've seen you at church. I know you believe in the words our priest tells us and yet you deny His involvement over our lives."

"The only demons upsetting this child are the ones you've instilled in him."

Mrs. Finney stood up from her chair, causing Chase to scoot back and cower in his. "I would never do anything to harm my youngest child," She put her hand on the table. "I should slap you for insinuating such a thing. I love my son-"

"Then why do you always talk about him like he's not in the room?" Rory's teeth gritted, he did not raise from his chair but his eyes threatened Mrs. Finney to sit back down. Chase was whispering under his breath, "The bathroom, the bathroom, quickly."

Mrs. Finney's eyes began to water. Slowly, she sat back down.

She wouldn't even look at Chase, her gaze was reserved for only Rory. She inhaled raggedly, hands folded and replied, "My son isn't here."

"Unbelievable," Rory growled.

"Please listen to what I have to say, Rory. You may not believe, but I've spoken to another one of your doctors in this facility. He also believes that Chase has lost himself to the demon's awful influence. I blame myself. If I can just be allowed to take him to church and have another baptism, he can be saved."

"You want to take a young man with hallucinations and extreme paranoia to a place where you plan to dunk him under Holy Water in an attempt to cleanse him of his mental illness?" Rory demanded with eyes narrowed.

"Even if we don't take him anywhere, the priest assured me that drinking Holy Water would also work." She shifted her weight to one side and moved her hand to her hip.

Rory stood from his seat and Mrs. Finney retreated her hand to her chest. "Listen here," Rory said. "You need to stop trying to push your son's condition into something it's not. You need to think logically for once in your life and realize that this isn't the work of some evil thing. What Chase has is a mental condition, not spiritual corruption. And what you are isn't a devout believer, but an over-intrusive woman who refuses to be wrong."

"If you're so sure it would fail, why don't you help me approve it and then see who is wrong?"

"Because something like that would traumatize Chase at best and make it so he won't trust anyone again at worst. If it was something Chase would want to try, that's the only time I would ever consider it."

"Well his opinion doesn't matter in this case," Mrs. Finney argued.

"How can you think his opinion- you know what, we're finished here." Rory reached his limit. His only thought was how he needed to get out of the room. He stormed out of the visiting room and told the caretaker waiting outside, "Escort Mrs. Finney out of the building, their visit is finished." Rory didn't wait for a response, he just kept storming towards the front door. He crossed paths with Eloise and Chase's brother on the way. He was sure Eloise asked where he was going, though he was too enraged to hear her. He answered her anyway.

"I'm going home. I can't stand another minute around that woman."

"What woman," Chase's brother inquired.

Rory turned to him, a bit of venom in his tone. "Your insufferable mother, that's who." When he realized the involuntary disdain he gave them, he added with the last of his patience, "Good day to you both." Rory turned towards his escape and hurried home as quickly as possible. He thought about his own son and couldn't imagine in a million years saying or doing half of the things to Junior what Mrs. Finney did to Chase.

"Dear, what's wrong?" Mrs. Figg asked her husband as he stormed into the house.

"Hello honey," He gave her a quick kiss before looking around. "Where's Junior?"

"He went to Bo's house to play," She told him. "Rory, did something happen at work?"

Rory sighed and started to pull off his tie. "Mrs. Finney came to visit again today."

"Today?" She mused. "Strange, she usually has book club on Wednesdays."

It was just like Ms. Figg to know everyone's gossip in town. "She came in demanding a baptism for her son."

"Is a baptism so wrong?" Mrs. Figg asked.

"It is when you're trying to use it as an alternative to modern medicine," Rory replied. "She didn't even care to look at Chase, honey. It was like he didn't even exist."

Mrs. Figg smiled a little. "You take the care of these patients so personally sometimes. I know how hard it was for you when Francine passed away."

"It was bound to happen," Rory muttered.

"You can't hide it from me," Mrs. Figg hugged him from behind. "I think it's wonderful that you feel so strongly for the patients. They need people who care like you do."

Rory turned to hold her. "I just can't stand that woman. That's all."

"I can't either," Mrs. Figg reminded him. "She is insufferable during Bible study. I sometimes wish I could have just one Sunday without her there."

Once Junior got home, they played a game together as a family, had dinner, then listened to the radio after sending Junior to bed.

Rory slept soundly with his wife in his arms, but he was dreading going back to work the next morning.

Once there he was immediately visited by the Head Doctor himself. "Rory I want you in my office immediately."

Rory snapped back to the present moment, noting how tired Dr. Von Ruck looked. Rory had no idea what it could be about, but he had the feeling as though it was something serious. Rory followed the doctor to his office. Von Ruck closed the door behind them. "Have a seat, Rory."

Rory obliged without hesitation. Von Ruck walked to his office chair, sat down, and folded his hands. "Can you explain to me what happened in the visiting room yesterday?"

"Why, what happened?" Rory asked. He was cut short with Von Ruck's hand motioning for him to stop.

Dr. Von Ruck began once more. "Please tell me what happened in the visiting room."

"Mrs. Finney refused to speak to Chase, she and I had an argument and I left the room."

"You left Chase alone with her?"

Rory felt a chill up his spine. "I told another caretaker to escort her out before I left."

"Do you remember who you asked to do that?"

Rory searched his memory for familiar faces, but he realized to his frustration that, besides Eloise, Rory didn't pay enough attention to the other caretakers to recall the name or the face. "He was a taller fella, nice hair. I don't really remember."

"The reason I ask, Rory, is because after you left Chase and Mrs. Finney alone, she attacked Chase and had to be escorted off the premises." Rory was at a loss for words. He looked to Von Ruck with several questions on his mind.

"Is Chase alright," Was his first question.

"He seems to be thanks to Dr. Bandit," Was Von Ruck's response.

Rory figured that if Eloise was good for anything, at least it was her work with Chase. "What did Mrs. Finney do to him?" He was, admittedly, more curious about this answer.

"She forced him to drink something in a vial. She refuses to tell anyone what it was."

Rory thought for a moment about their conversation. He wondered if she somehow had some Holy Water with her. Well, if anything, she'll now realize that the Holy Water wasn't going to fix anything. Maybe now he wouldn't have to listen to her anymore. That was, if he still had a job. "What's going to happen to me?" This was, to him, the most important question.

"Well, we aren't sure about that yet. You are a valuable member of the team, but we also can't have your mistake happen again."

"I swear it won't happen again," Rory insisted. "I would never purposefully put a patient in danger, you know that."

Dr. Von Ruck nodded. "Be extra careful with Chase today," He told Rory. "We have no way of knowing what sort of impact this situation has had on the boy."

Rory headed over to Chase's room. The boy was already awake, but he was quiet. Rory opened the door slower than usual. Chase didn't move. Strange, he was usually so jumpy. The kid laid there, and once again Rory was reminded of the boy that was fighting in that mind. "Chase," He called out to him.

Chase's eyes looked down to the door. He didn't respond. Instead, slowly, he sat up in bed. Somehow, this was more alarming to Rory than any of Chase's freak-outs. "Hey, Chase. It's time for breakfast."

Chase didn't respond. He just looked down at his bed. Chase's face then scrunched up, and he hid his face in the palms of his hands. He sniffed, his shoulders heaving.

Rory remembered Chase having days like this when he first started to take his medicine. There were strange, silent moments of clarity. He would have them rarely, and though Rory would feel a bit of relief, like seeing a step of progress, seeing the kid cry like that after being attacked by his mother made it hard for Rory to breathe. "I can't see them," Chase's voice squeaked.

"Isn't that a good thing?" Rory offered.

Chase shook his head. "You don't understand," He whispered. Rory waited for him to continue, but Chase never said anything to clarify. Rory sighed deeply.

"Chase," Rory said. "I'm sorry for what happened with… For what happened yesterday. How do you feel? Any pain?" Chase put his hands down on his lap and shook his head. Rory nodded, "That's good." Rory was aware that he had other patients he hadn't woken up yet. But he had to get Chase to eat breakfast. Still, Rory didn't feel like forcing Chase to do anything at the moment. Rory thought of his wife and his son. A real mother would have never done something so awful to their son. "I can see you're not ready to go eat yet. So how about I come back after a little while and I can see if I can't bring breakfast to you. How does that sound?"

Chase was silent for a moment. "Okay," He whispered.

Rory nodded and closed the door behind him. He got the other patients ready to start their days before making his way to the cafeteria to get Chase's food. He wondered if he would be able to get much out of Chase with him the way he was. Even on the days he was calm, he was never very cooperative. His mother must have terrified him enough to wake him up from whatever mental cloudiness he usually lived in. It didn't excuse what she did, but Rory thought maybe he could use this as an opportunity to ask a few questions. Rory hated to admit it, but Eloise probably knew better what questions to ask. There was a lot about Chase that no one knew about. He was apparently perfectly normal until around his teenage years. Well, Eloise was off so Rory would have to do his best.

He snuck in the breakfast. "I brought coffee," He told Chase. "Black, just how you like it."

Chase remained still, sitting on the bed. He raised his eyes to Rory's voice. His gaze darted around once or twice, but he looked straight at Rory most of the time. At the smell of coffee, his shoulders relaxed.

"Can I sit on the bed with you?" Rory asked. He knew he would have to clean the bed sheets to hide the evidence of the food before he left. Letting the patients eat in their room wasn't a huge deal, but Rory also didn't want to explain himself. Chase nodded.

Rory sat on the foot of the bed and gave Chase his food which had his medicine mixed with it before setting the coffee on the nightstand beside him. He let Chase get comfortable before he started to speak. "Chase, do you know who I am?"

Chase refused to make eye contact. There were a few seconds before he muttered, "I think so."

"You call me Wiggy."

Chase's face scrunched again. The grip on his spoon tightened.

Rory turned himself towards Chase a little bit. "Do you know Eloise?" He asked.

Chase scooped up a bit of food, but kept it on the plate. He started to hum a few bars of a familiar song. Rory tried to place where he's heard it. Chase stopped humming and ate a bit more.

Rory decided to drop the questions about Eloise. "Do you remember any family members or siblings?" He asked.

Chase kept eating. There was a long pause. He sighed, then shook his head. Rory could see the slight frustration in Chase's expression, as though he was either upset that he couldn't remember or upset Rory kept asking him questions. Rory looked down to Chase's food which was already nearly gone. Chase took a few sips of his coffee. Rory fidgeted his fingers. "Chase, what can you tell me about the broken door you always talk about?"

Chase lost his grip on his spoon. He sat there, staring at his plate. Rory immediately regretted trying to bring it up. "Forget I asked," He implored.

"I broke the door," He admitted.

"No really, you don't have to relive it," Rory insisted, seeing how upset Chase was beginning to feel.

"I broke the washer," Chase continued. "I broke the fence. I broke the car. I broke them. I broke everything. I broke the family." Tears cascaded from his eyes. Rory kept trying to quiet him down. "Just close your eyes and forget I'm here."

"I keep trying but I can't see them anymore!" Chase screamed. Rory fell silent. Chase clutched his head, the rest of his coffee spilled on the floor but Rory didn't dare make a move to pick it up.

"But the shadows," Chase whispered. "The shadows are still there. Whispering. Grabbing me, sneaking behind me, touching me, taking me, s-strangling me."

Rory slowly put up his hands. "I'm not going to touch you," He whispered. "But Chase, try to look at me. Try to see me. I'm real. I'm here. I'm trying to help you."

Chase wouldn't respond. He started to rock back and forth. Rory imagined that Chase's medicine would start kicking in at this time. His eyes weren't darting around, so the hallucinations must have stopped. Chase refused to look at the space around him. Rory didn't blame him. For the first time Rory wondered what was scariest, the hallucinations Chase saw every day or the place Chace saw he was at in during the moments he could see clearly.

No matter how he tried, he couldn't get chase to willingly leave his room. Rory didn't want to force him, either. What a day to be Eloise's day off. The evening shift would have to be filled by the fill-in caretaker. Rory called people like them 'temps' for short. He thought fondly of what Francine said about them. "Walking clipboards," She called them. Rory smiled a little. He missed her. She was always crude and unapologetic and said whatever was on her mind. He wished he could have been the one to be with her when she passed away. Instead it was one of the 'Walking clipboards.'

Rory thought about asking to call Eloise to come in, but he knew it would be unsettling for him to call her at home. She knew he didn't like her. Even still, Rory wasn't sure that whoever was assigned to Chase could do a good job looking after him. As it was nearing his shift, he decided to have a talk with whatever temp was filling in to see if Rory couldn't at least give the temp a little advice in caring for the kid.

"Caleb Stone," He read off of the schedule. Rory had no clue what this guy looked like. He decided to wait until this Dr. Stone arrived. At last Rory spotted him. He was a tall fella, short black hair combed to the side.

"Dr. Figg, what are you still doing here? I'm supposed to take over your shift."

"Yes, that's what I wanted to talk to you about," Rory revealed.

Dr. Stone shifted his weight. "Is something wrong?"

"You probably heard. The whole asylum is buzzing about how Chase had a situation with a visitor yesterday. As a result, he doesn't want to leave his room. Don't force him."

Dr. Stone nodded his head, "Naturally. I'll try to be as unobtrusive as possible."

Rory stared him down. "Have we met before?"

"A few times," Dr. Stone conceded. "We do work in the same facility."

"How long have you worked here?" Rory asked.

"Is this an interrogation?" Dr. Stone raised an eyebrow.

"Think of it as an interview," Rory responded. "I just think it's a shame we work together and yet I don't know a thing about you."

Dr. Stone smiled lightly. "Well if it's friendship you're looking after, you only had to ask. To answer your question, I've been here for only a few months. I transferred here from another job. I was given a nice little place with my wife downtown. You're welcome to come by sometime, we're getting work done."

"We'll see," Rory lied. He didn't want to know this man's entire life story. Maybe Chase would be fine, the guy seemed friendly enough. "Well, I'd love to chat more but I have to go home to my wife."

Rory got home at last, but his mind stayed at work. He didn't know how to place it, but he just kept feeling like something was wrong. He watched a movie with his family after dinner and held his wife close when they got into bed.

That morning, his alarm radio woke him at five, like every day. He had one hour to get to work, like every day. He got dressed and ready, able to get to the asylum and clock in about three minutes early, like every day. However, something about this day was different. He felt it as he woke up all the other patients. He felt it as he walked down the long hallway to Chase's room. He saw it when he opened the door.

"Help!" He cried down the hallway. "Someone help for the love of Almighty!" Four other caretakers rushed to Rory's aid only to see what he saw in the room.

Chase sat there in puke and bile, still and cold. He was stiff and pale, his eyes open but glazed over. Rory couldn't stop shaking. Was it despair? Perhaps fear? Rory knew there was likely a mix of that within his chest, but what rose beyond all of it was rage.

Rory heard Von Ruck in the other room calling Chase's brother and aunt. The police apprehended Mrs. Finney for questioning. The popular belief was that she poisoned him, but as much as Rory hated Mrs. Finney, he didn't suspect her at all.

An officer came to Rory and asked him about anything he might know. "It's documented that you were one of the last people to see him alive," The policeman reminded him.

"The person you want to talk about is Caleb Stone," Rory told him. "He was the last person who saw Chase alive."

"Doctor, we are interviewing anyone who would have had contact with Chase. Please just answer my questions and leave the interrogation to us."

Frustrated, Rory answered all the questions. When Eloise arrived, she was more devastated than anyone. Rory practically felt guilty. He also noticed, however, how much she leaned on Chase's brother for comfort.

The following day was Rory's day off, but he came in for an impromptu visit to have a conversation with Dr. Caleb Stone. Rory had to remain generally unseen, unless Von Ruck would want to know why he was here on his day off. Rory read the schedule and saw Dr. Caleb Stone's name. Rory hurried down the hallway until he could see the back of a tall fella. "Dr. Stone," Rory called out to him. "I need to speak with you."

The doctor turned around to look Rory's way. "Dr. Figg? Is there something you need to see me about?"

Rory stopped dead, his feet like magnets to the floor beneath him. As though his shadow became the tar to ensnare and petrify him. The man standing before Rory, though he was tall and his black hair combed neatly, looked otherwise nothing like the man Rory spoke with the night before Chase was murdered. "Stone?" Rory asked to make sure. "You are Dr. Caleb Stone?"

"Yes, my name is Dr. Caleb Stone," He confirmed.

"Are you the only Dr. Caleb Stone that works here?"

Dr. Stone raised an eyebrow. "Yes?" He replied. "Dr. Figg, are you feeling alright?"

Rory's gaze fell to the ground. He put a hand to his forehead. He closed his eyes and gritted his teeth. "Nothing, nevermind."

Rory hurried back to his car and sat in it for a while, trying to think of all the events that happened in the past few days. In the end, he couldn't come to any conclusion about what it all meant. "I need a vacation," He decided.

MY ONLY FRIEND

Maybe it isn't fair to say I've never had any friends growing up. There were certainly people who I considered friends for a time, but in hindsight never acted much like a friend at all. There were people who were nice to me, but they would never stay long. They would rather go outside at recess or after school and play football or kickball or any other sort of variation of taking balls or pucks from place to place. I couldn't kick a ball. I couldn't really throw one, either. The kids got annoyed with how long it took for the teachers to get my wheelchair on and off the bus at field trips. The teachers would sit near me or push me around most of the time, as though I needed a constant chaperone. Having them around me all the time was always awkward. I never knew what to talk about.

I remember the day I met him. I was alone in my room. Mom was making dinner, talking to one of my older sisters. It was safe to say I was truly alone when in my room. No one at home really came to see me unless they needed something or it was time to eat. I imagined it was because they found it hard to talk to me, but imagine how I felt. No one really knew how to talk to me. It wasn't so hard.

"Hey."

I turned to look at my bed. There he sat, a cheeky grin on his face, but I couldn't quite make out anything else.

"Hey," I replied.

"What's with the wheels?" He asked.

"Cerebral Palsy," I admitted.

He tilted his head to the side. "What's that?"

"For me it just means that I can't make any friends," I sighed. "I either make people uncomfortable or people just want to be friends with me to seem like a good person when they don't even know anything about me."

He tilted his head to the other side. "What do you like to do?"

I smiled a little at my bed. The boy was there, kicking his legs. Or maybe he didn't have legs. No, he definitely had legs, and he was definitely kicking them. "I like to draw," I told him. "Though I'm not all that good at it yet. I want to be an animator someday."

"Do you like cartoons then?" He asked.

"I love them," I told him. "I watch them every time I can

manage to get the living room by myself. Mom says if I bring my grades up, she'll install a television in my room. I can't really tell if it's to reward me or so that there are less times that she has to worry about interacting with me."

"I'm sure it's to reward you," the boy said.

"You think so?" I asked.

"Sure," He shrugged. "I mean, you're the most behaved child. Why shouldn't you get your own T.V.?"

I grinned, then I heard mother coming down the stairs to my room. She knocked and opened the door. "Ash, It's time for dinner. Do you want me to help you upstairs?"

"I'll be right up, mom," I assured her. "I think I have the strength to click the 'forward' button up the ramp."

Mom sighed, "I just wanted to be sure. See you up there then." She left my door open and I turned back to see that the boy was gone. Still, I knew that we would talk another time. I then realized that I never asked for his name. I spent the rest of the evening trying to think of what his name would be.

The very next day, I was alone in my room again. "Hello Ash," the boy greeted from my bed.

"Hello Leigh," I replied.

I had countless conversations with Leigh almost every day. The best part about having Leigh as a friend was that we could just talk. There was no pressure of wanting to play or any awkward feelings. Some days, when I was frustrated at school, he would listen to me vent. When there was something that I needed to say to someone else, Leigh and I would rehearse the conversation. Leigh always knew what I needed to hear. Leigh was always there when I needed him. I didn't tell anyone about Leigh. He was a secret that I kept to myself.

Eventually, I did get the television in my room. I would watch it and sketch into the countless notebooks I could get a hold of. Even then, when I felt lonely, I would occasionally ask Leigh how he liked the show we were watching. I still spoke with Leigh a few times a week or more depending on how bad school was.

"Hello."

Someone I had never seen in school before came up to me during recess. I was against the building, reading a book, but the unfamiliar voice called me from my escape. I put my book down to address them.

95

"I'm sorry," This guy said to me. "Today is my first day in a new school and I thought we might be able to talk. My name is Jake."

I looked him over. When my eyes made it to his legs, I noticed that one was missing and the other was in a plastic brace. He carried crutches under his arms. "What happened to your legs?" I asked.

"Cancer," He admitted. "What happened to yours?"

We talked through recess and on every break until we went home. We kept talking together every day at school and then he came to visit my house during the summer. I started speaking to Leigh less and less. Over the span of a year or two, the boy named Jake became my best friend and I all but forgot about Leigh.

Years went by. Jake and I were no longer in school. I became an animator for a small short film company. After so long, I still never forgot about Leigh. I told Jake about him and he suggested that I animate a short film about him, so I did. I created new characters for Leigh to interact with. Not only did my work approve of him, but so did an audience of people all over the world. In the end, I was able to keep living on because I had someone like him to talk to. In return, I got to help him exist in more than just my mind. To this day, I still consider Leigh to be my very first friend.

INTRUDER

Mercedes knew where everything was in her house. She knew how many steps it took to get to the grocery store. She knew what made every sound. All she needed was her walking stick to get to anywhere she needed to go on her block. Daphne would drive her everywhere else. Mercedes lived alone in her little house for nearly twelve years. The library where she worked was 67 steps to the left of the trailer park where her house was. The grocery store was 93 steps, turn right, and another 12 steps away.

Mercedes knew everyone that lived in the park and in the few blocks within walking distance. She lived a stable, comforting, predictable life. That's why she was suddenly alarmed when late at night she heard something shift in her living room. She grabbed her phone which always sat at arm's length on her nightstand and told the voice command as quietly as possible to 'Call Daphne.'

A tired, mumbling voice answered the phone. "Mercedes? It's four in the morning."

"Daphne, someone is in my house," She whispered. "Hurry and come over, please."

"Did you call the police?" Daphne asked, now less asleep.

"Not yet," Mercedes confessed.

"Why not? Are you hiding? Tell me what's going on."

Mercedes strained to hear anything else, but everything was silent. "I'm not hiding. I don't hear anything anymore but will you please still come by? It could be a raccoon or something in the kitchen."

Daphne moaned, but conceded. "Alright, alright. I'll be there in five minutes."

True to her word, Daphne came to Mercedes' house. Mercedes knew it was her because Daphne was the only person that had a spare key. Daphne was quietly looking around the living room as she wandered in. Mercedes could hear the small creaks of her friend's steps. Mercedes feared that she would hear Daphne cry out or some other scuffle, but she just heard her friend call out, "Mercedes?"

"I'm in my room, Daphne," Mercedes replied. "Did you see anything?"

"There's not a hair out of place," Daphne reported. "Are you sure you heard the noise inside and not outside?"

"You know that my hearing is nearly perfect," Mercedes defended. "But maybe I was dreaming it or something. Anyway, thank you for checking up on me regardless."

"Of course I would, girl," Daphne responded with a bit more liveliness before falling back into a slumbering murmur. "Just next time maybe make sure it's not a dream. Also, you should call the police if you really think it's an intruder. Not much that a tiny woman like me can do."

Mercedes gave her friend a nod. "Still, I'm glad to know that you would come out so late to rescue me. You really are a great friend."

"You just need to take my advice more often," Daphne laughed. "Things would go a lot more smoothly if you weren't notoriously stubborn."

"You are just as stubborn," Mercedes laughed back. "That's why we became friends."

Daphne went back home to get some sleep. She made sure to lock the door behind her. Mercedes was able to sleep the rest of the night, but she still couldn't help but feel as though she was being watched. The unmistakable feeling of eyes peering into ones being was hitting her and she had no idea why.

The next morning, Mercedes went to work. She read stories to the smaller children almost every day. She ran her finger along the brail and told the children what it read. She took pleasure in giving every character a voice and she enjoyed pausing in dramatic moments to give the children a bit more thrill. She knew they were waiting in anticipation. She could feel their eager eyes watching her read. Mercedes loved her job at the library. She felt as though she was doing some good while reading to children. She would also teach other blind children how to read in brail so they didn't have to miss out on their favorite fairytales and fantasies.

After work, Mercedes walks to the market. She knew where every item was at the grocer. Once she gathered what she needed, she would either go to Daphne's house or she would go home and read. Mercedes placed her food in the fridge. She set everything in the exact spot, so when the back of her hand hit a jar of mayonnaise, Mercedes froze. She stood still, trying to see if she could hear anyone nearby.

The clock over her kitchen counter 'ticked' rhythmically. Slowly, she reached to touch the hands of the clock. It read 6:45 PM. Mercedes still didn't hear anything, so she placed the mayonnaise where it should be and closed the fridge. Mercedes turned on her living room radio and turned the volume down low. She grabbed a book from her bookshelf, cuddled into her couch, and started to read.

'Creeeeak.'

Mercedes gasped and held the book to her chest. She froze and listened, facing down the hallway where her bedroom door was. She always kept her doors closed when she was out. She remembered vividly that she closed it. Mercedes fumbled for the phone. She wanted to call Daphne first, but she knew Daphne wanted her to call the police. Mercedes thought about the police coming in and moving things, and if they didn't find anything, she worried about being charged for a false report. She never had need for the police before, but she heard stories about things like that happening. Her job at the library barely paid for her bills, she wouldn't be able to afford a ticket. But was it worth possibly her life? Well, if someone was in the house, they haven't killed her yet.

She called Daphne.

"Daphne, can you come over?"

"I thought you were too tired from work to have company," Daphne reminded her.

"Right, but I just miss you and would like for you to come over now, please," Mercedes pleaded.

Daphne sighed, "I was watching television."

"You can do that here. I got the television for my guests and it's just sitting here gathering dust."

"Alright, I'll be right over. Are you feeling alright?" Daphne asked.

"I'm fine," Mercedes lied.

When Daphne arrived, she knocked lightly on the door and helped herself in. "It's just me, Mercedes."

"I know," Mercedes replied.

"Okay, I thought I saw you jump when I knocked on the door so I wanted to make sure."

Mercedes heard the floor creak, then a 'click' as the television started to rave about buying a new car at any local dealer near you. Mercedes cleared her throat. "Daphne, could you do me a favor and tell me if my bedroom door is opened or closed?"

"Sure," There was more creaking and a 'click.' Mercedes was reminded that it had been a while since she bought more light bulbs and hoped that her friend could still see down the hallway. "The door is closed," She confirmed.

Mercedes felt a chill. "Are any of the other doors open down that hallway?"

"Nope, all the doors are closed. Why do you ask?"

"Daphne, I have one more favor to ask."

"I thought we were going to watch television," Daphne reminded.

"I know, but I just have one more thing, it won't take long," Mercedes promised. "Will you check and see if you see anyone in any of the rooms?"

The air in the room tensed. Mercedes listened to the radio and television fight for attention while the clock in the kitchen rhythmically ticked in the background. Daphne made no sound for what felt like moments.

"Do you think there's someone in the house?"

Mercedes pursed her lips. "Maybe."

"Mercedes, that's dangerous, why didn't you call the police?"

"We can handle it," Mercedes argued.

"Two women, one very small and the other blind, cannot handle an intruder in your house."

"They're obviously scared enough to not make noises when you're around," Mercedes pointed out. "Just take a quick look in each room Daphne, please, it'll make me feel better."

Daphne let out an exasperated sigh. "Fine. But if there is someone I'm running out of this house and calling the police immediately and you better be right behind me because I'm not coming back for you."

"Fair deal," Mercedes replied.

Mercedes turned off the radio, but the television still provided its backup noise. She could hear the light 'thuds' of footsteps and the occasional creak of the floor. Mercedes knew when Daphne passed her restroom door when it made what Mercedes called the 'question creak.' It ended in a high note, as though it wasn't sure of itself. The farthest door, her bedroom, was the first to be checked. Mercedes waited, holding her breath, listening to every shuffle, every creak, every sigh.

Both girls were dead quiet. Mercedes didn't want to startle

Daphne as she searched and Daphne didn't want anyone else that could be in the house know where she was. Room after room, door after door, Daphne was making her way closer to the living room, back to Mercedes. The more she searched, the braver she must have felt, as Mercedes noticed Daphne making noises a bit more liberally. The floorboards creaked quicker, the small taps and shuffles became thumps and screeches. "There's nobody here," Daphne called out at last.

"Are you sure?" Mercedes called back.

"Mercedes, I looked through every nook and cranny of every room, I'm pretty sure."

"Did you put back everything you moved?"

"Yes, Mercedes, I put back everything I moved. It's like I was never there. Now that we're done, can we please watch some television?"

The next few hours, Mercedes read on her couch while Daphne sat across the room watching television. Mercedes liked these moments, just having Daphne in the same room was comforting. They didn't have to be enjoying the same thing, Mercedes just liked having her friend there with her. Daphne would explain to Mercedes what happened on the television occasionally, and just as often Mercedes would tell Daphne what she was reading.

Time went on and as Mercedes began to start nodding off on her couch, Daphne clicked off the television. "I think it's time for me to go to bed. Will you be okay now, Mercedes?"

"I'm alright now, thank you Daphne," Mercedes obliged. "You are the best."

"That is true," Daphne replied. "But next time, I mean it. Call the police if it happens again."

"Alright, I'm sorry," Mercedes conceded.

Mercedes was sound asleep. Her dreams were filled with music and voices of people she knew. She felt the familiar scene of the library. She heard children laughing and a book in the fingertips of her left hand. She trailed the right where the bookshelf was, skimming her fingers through the titles. The names she was reading were skewed, but she didn't notice anything wrong. 'The Prince Hess and the Paper,' 'War and Doves,' and 'Alice Wonder Wonder.' She heard her own voice telling a story. The children continued to talk and laugh. "Do you want a banana smoothie?" She heard Daphne ask.

'Creeeeeeeeak?'

Everything went numb. Everything went silent. Mercedes remained perfectly still, listening. She could hear the faint ticking of the clock in the kitchen. The wind outside made leaves rustle and the wind chimes jingle next door.

'Thump.'

Mercedes fumbled for the phone on her nightstand.

'Thump.'

She covered the speaker on her phone and put it on silent. Her fingers shook with every tap of her screen. Without the sound of the phone letting her know it registered her touch, she had no way of knowing if she was dialing on the phone keypad.

'Thump. Crick.'

Mercedes covered her head under the blankets. She pressed the phone to her ear. She was trembling, listening in terror for the 'click' and 'creak' of her bedroom door.

"Hello this is the Gainesville County Police are you in a safe place?"

Mercedes feared cracking the phone with her grip. "No." She whispered. "Help."

She heard the woman on the phone shift her weight. "We're pinpointing your location from your phone miss, stay on the line with me as long as you can. Can you move to somewhere safe?"

'Click.'

"Miss? Can you hear me? Can you describe your situation?"

"They're in my house," She whispered. "Outside my r-,"

'Creeeeak.'

Mercedes hung up the phone as quickly as she could. She begged for the intruder to see just the blanket and leave. She prayed the police would get there fast. Every second was a gamble on her life. The hand around her phone was cramping. She was frozen, listening for any noises. She knew they were in the room, staring at her. Still. Silent. Staring.

Mercedes tried to breathe slowly. Her nose was running but she dared not sniff it. Her tears tickled her cheek but she dared not wipe it away.

She heard a couple car engines approach and go silent in front of her house. She felt hope. She heard footprints surround the trailer. A single set of footprints thudded their way to the front door. She heard the front doorknob jiggle and click. 'screeeee' went the front door. Mercedes let go of the phone and in a wave of bravery she threw the covers down from her head and screamed, "I'm in here!"

Relief swept over her as she heard the growing sound of boots making their way to her room. She heard the 'Creeeak?' Then 'click' and 'Creeak.'

"Are you hurt ma'am? Where's the intruder?"

"I don't know, I'm blind," She explained. "But I heard them, they were just in this room."

She heard 'clunks' and 'scritch' and 'thumps' as the officer checked every place in her room. She heard his shoes come to the bed and she felt a light incline and a 'thump' as he got to his knees. "Any idea who they were, Ma'am?"

"They're footprints are too heavy for anyone I might know," Mercedes admitted. "I have no idea who it could be."

"But we're looking for someone large," The officer gathered. "We'll investigate the area a bit more. Would you like to have someone here with you while we search?"

"Yes please," Mercedes requested. "Please try to put everything back where it was, I can't find my way around otherwise."

Mercedes heard static and then the officer started speaking quickly. After a moment, a muffled voice replied. Mercedes waited for them to search, all the while trying to think of how the intruder could have closed her door without her knowing.

Moments passed by, and Mercedes felt the wave of fatigue creep onto her once more now that the danger seemed to have passed. Still, she was worried. What would the police think if the intruder wasn't caught? She was anxious over everything they moved. The same officer from before walked back into the room.

"We couldn't find the intruder, ma'am. Are you sure they were here?"

"I have no doubt in my mind," Mercedes replied.

"We'll lock up before we leave. If they show up again don't hesitate to call us. If I can offer some advice?"

Mercedes nodded.

"Have something at your bedside to defend yourself. If you can afford it, maybe also adopt a service dog. They can help you around the house and alert you if there are any intruders."

"Yes sir, thank you," Mercedes responded.

She had a hard time sleeping the rest of the night. She kept straining to hear anything out of the ordinary, but all she heard the rest of the night was the settling of the house and the faint ticking of the kitchen clock.

Throughout the next couple days, Mercedes would find things out of place. She believed it must have been the officers and she would put the things back where they belonged. Occasionally, however, she thought she moved something back in its place only to find where it was before.

"Why do you have a baseball bat by your bed?" Daphne asked one day as she came to visit.

"Just in case the intruder returns," Mercedes replied. "I haven't heard them since I called the police, but I can't be too careful. I was also thinking of getting a dog."

"You're allergic to fur," Daphne reminded her.

"Yes, but there are dogs that are supposed to be okay for people that are allergic."

"Mercedes, if there is someone who can come into your house so easily, have you thought about moving out?"

"Daphne, think about how that would upset every part of my life," Mercedes reminded her friend. "I would either have to be walking distance from the library or someone would have to be willing to drive me there almost every day. I would have to get familiar with an entirely different layout. There is no need to go so drastic if we can only find and catch the intruder."

"I suppose," Daphne sighed. "I just get worried. You could stay with me until you found somewhere else to live."

"Well, I haven't even heard them in the house in days. Maybe the problem fixed itself."

The night was calm and still. The distant ticking of the kitchen clock was all Mercedes could hear. She laid in her bed, cuddled up to her blankets. The night air was beginning to chill. Small critters ran and nestled into the leaves that sprinkled the lawn outside. Mercedes fell asleep thinking about Daphne and the library. She revisited past memories of feeling the ocean spray on her face and the sand beneath her feet. Her ears were remembering old songs and the voices of High School friends. Book quotes recited in her mind in the form of a melody encapsulating her childhood.

'Creeeeeeeeak?'

Mercedes' body jerked awake.

'Thump. Crik.'

She reached for the bat, it's unfamiliar cold presence furthering her departure from her cozy sleep. She pulled the bat into the covers with her and waited.

'Click. Creeeeeeeak.'

Her grip on the bat tightened. She kept lying down, pretending to be asleep, waiting for the footsteps that would come up to her. Her muscles were tense, poised like a viper, ready to spring into action.

However, her body became bone stiff at the sound of the breathing. A light, gentle, audible wheezing right behind her.

Against her ear.

Mercedes' scream was louder than she thought she could manage. She swung the covers and the bat. She sprung up and kept swinging in every direction she thought she heard noise. She backed up to her door. Her back hit cold wood. With one hand, she swung open the door. She dropped the bat and ran. In her panic, she ran into a desk. The desk wasn't supposed to be blocking the hallway. The intruder was trying to slow her down. She heard rapid footsteps behind her. 'Creeeak?'

There was no time. She tipped the desk over and ran to the front door. She flung the door open and ran down the porch steps, screaming into the cold, dead night. She ran to Daphne's trailer and banged on the door as hard as she could.

"Mercedes, what's going on?"

"Quickly, Its gaining!" She cried. Daphne ushered her in and closed the door.

Mercedes spent the night with Daphne. That morning, she and Daphne went to look for clues to who was coming after her. There was a tipped over desk and nothing else out of place. After days of staying with Daphne, they found a small place for Mercedes to live. She had to start taking the city bus as part of her routine.

Ever since Mercedes moved out, she has had no issues with intruders in her new place or in any place since. Mercedes would check the news and see if anyone that may have been the intruder was ever caught, but for her whole life, she was never sure they were ever found. Sometimes, in the moments that she doubted herself the most, she wondered if there was a chance that she imagined the whole thing.

Years passed. Daphne came to visit, and it had been so long since she lived in the old house that Mercedes nearly forgot all about it. But as they drank tea and reminisced about old times, Daphne fell silent. "Do you remember the old house you lived in?" She asked.

Mercedes nodded, "Oh yes, I do."

Daphne's cup clinked onto the tray. "Remember when you asked me to look around for you and I told you that nothing was out of place?" Mercedes felt her hair stand on end. "Well I may have lied to you, I'm sorry. I just didn't want you to worry."

"What do you mean?" Mercedes demanded.

"In your bedroom, there was a stain in the carpet by the window, and the window was wide open. It looked like an ink stain. I'm not sure, only that it was black and a little bit of it was on the wall under the window. It seemed like nothing to me at the time, but recently I kept thinking about it and realized I should have brought it up. I just didn't want to alarm you."

"Well now I wish you never did," Mercedes cried. "What was it, who opened my window, what else could have been wandering around in my house without me knowing?"

"I'm sorry, I don't know," Daphne replied. "I guess it's just one mystery that will never be solved."

RUN

Ophelia loved her family. She loved how her adopted father would tuck her in and how he would always ask her if she needed anything. She loved how her adopted mother sang to her and told her stories. Whenever Ophelia would cry, they would comfort her. Whenever she was hurt, they would always make it better. She was their porcelain child, a very sick girl, but they spent every spare moment they could to let her know she was loved. The older Ophelia got, however, the more she wanted to meet other children. Sometimes her parents were so protective that she couldn't spend a moment alone. She loved her family, but sometimes when they were asleep, she would sneak outside to enjoy a small moment of freedom.

She was no older than five and still trying to walk without scraping her shoes on the pavement. She had to make sure not to fall or she would be in a lot of trouble. Ophelia knew every family on the block, so in her mind she knew the entire world. Because of this truth in her mind, she was curious about a man she had never seen before, mumbling to himself in the alleyway between the Jones' house and the corner store. "Hello," She called to the mumbling man. "Are you okay?"

The man swiftly spun to face her. His emerald eyes fixed upon this pale, pink-eyed little girl. Even as he stood before her, Ophelia didn't shy away.

"What are you doing out here little girl, and in the middle of the night?" The man's raspy voice called to her.

"What were you mumbling about?" Ophelia tilted her head.

The man straightened out his long, black trench coat. "Oh, I was just..." He trailed off. "Where are your parents?"

"They're sleeping at home," Ophelia answered. "But they don't know I'm outside. Please don't tell them."

"You should run home. It's really dangerous for you to be outside all by yourself," The man explained.

"I'm not by myself," She reminded him. "You're here too."

The man paused. "I'm a stranger. You shouldn't trust strangers."

"Why?" She asked.

"You're not afraid of me at all," The man mused.

"Do I have to be?" Ophelia wondered.

After a few seconds of silence, the man's raspy voice let out an amused chuckle. "What's your name, sweetheart?"

"Ophelia," She replied.

"Well Ophelia, I think I have something to give you." The man pulled a blue backpack from his shoulders. He set it onto the floor and crouched down in front of it. Ophelia could see papers with blue squares on them and books inside as the man in the long jacket rummaged to the bottom of the backpack. "Here he is," The man commented as he pulled out a doll. Ophelia looked at the brown doll with two different sized button eyes and black silky hair.

"Is that doll for me?" Ophelia asked.

The man zipped up his backpack and rested on one knee. He kept his gaze on the little girl. "Listen Ophelia. This doll is more than just a toy. He is a lost soul looking for a place to belong. If you treat him with love, he will protect you. Can you promise me that you will give him a place to belong?"

Ophelia nodded fervently. "Uh-huh, I promise."

"Okay," The man held out the doll for Ophelia. She took the doll and held it close to her. She felt a strange emotion as she held the doll, as though it were filling up a hole or answering a question that she never thought to ask but always wondered.

"Now, I'm going to walk you home," The man said. "Once you get home, you have to not run around by yourself after dark anymore. If I see you out here alone again then I will tell your parents."

Ophelia's eyes widened. "No please don't tell them!" She begged.

"I'll keep it a secret," The man promised. "As long as you never do it again."

Ophelia huffed, "Okay," She mumbled.

The man in the trench coat followed Ophelia home. He waited for her to go back inside. She waved at him from the window. He smiled and waved back before putting his hands in his pockets and walking away.

Ophelia never wandered out at night alone again, afraid that if the man in the trench coat saw her again then he would tell on her. She kept the little doll that the man gave her. The little girl held the doll close to her chest every night. She started to take him everywhere she went. She was never without the burlap doll. Since the doll was given to her on the last night she ever ran away at night, Ophelia decided to name her new friend 'Runner.'

MIDNIGHT RIDE

Reid remembered when he was very young how his father used to take him out on midnight rides around the neighborhood on his motorcycle. It was famously known among Reid's family and friends that he could never stay awake when riding in any vehicle. He was alright when he was driving, but as a passenger the smooth rush of the wind and the low rumble of the ground beneath him combined with the light bumping was enough to lull Reid to sleep.

The world seemed to slow down at night, Reid mused. He stood on his front porch, taking in the sweet, cool breeze. 'Like whispers from the stars,' He thought as he witnessed the sky communicate with twinkling lights.

"Reid, don't you have work in the morning?" His mother called from inside. "Maybe you should get into bed."

"Yeah," Reid conceded. "That's probably for the best."

"I made some tacos in the kitchen if you want one."

"Yes please," He grinned. "I'll be inside after I finish this smoke, I promise."

Reid's mother retreated back into the warm house. Reid looked back up at the sky. He had nearly forgotten the smoke in his hand before he needed an excuse to stay out a bit longer. He tapped the ash away and watched the embers burn the paper as though it were marking nearer to the end of time itself. He closed his eyes to focus on the song of the cicadas, the rustling of leaves, and the sound of the distant train.

Wait.

Reid opened his eyes. "Wait, there are no train tracks in this town," He muttered. He listened in harder. The sound was clearly a train, but something was bizarre, whether it be the sheer absurdity of a train being within hearing distance or something else. He had the urge to investigate, but the call of his mother's tacos and the call of tomorrow's responsibilities stilled his adventuring heart. If he heard it again, he decided, then he would investigate.

His job wasn't difficult to do, but he felt as though the day was fighting through a lake of sap whenever he was there. He had nothing to do except for the same menial tasks day after day, working for the canning factory, making cans and making more cans and still more cans. Reid celebrated surviving his shift with some partying. He and some friends of his went to the 8-Ball Club and was driven home wasted. Donovan was the designated driver. He took everyone home, Reid being the last. As expected, he was fast asleep. "Reid," Donovan nudged his friend. "Reid, get up. You're home."

"No, I'm sleeping," Reid slurred.

Donovan laughed, "Come on man get up. I gotta go home, dude."

Reid rubbed at his eyes. He started to sit up in his seat when he heard the familiar uncanny whistle. "Donovan what's that train sound?"

"There's no train sound Reid," Donovan replied as though he were speaking to a toddler.

"No but can't you hear it? There's a train, it's whistling."

"Reid, you need to go to bed. Come on, or I'll have to get your mom to help me and she would be livid if I had to wake her up to get your drunken butt inside."

The whistle persisted. "Donovan I think, you shhhh- you should go see what the thing is with me."

"We'll go see the thing tomorrow," Donovan got out of the car and opened Reid's door.

"That would be too late, Donovan. We'll miss the train."

"What train?" Donovan asked. "There is no train, you're just hearing whistles in your head. Just go to bed Reid, come on. You might not have to work tomorrow, but I do."

Defeated, Reid rolled his head Donovan's way and gave him a sigh with a fragrance of rum. "Okay fine, I'll go since you're bein' a big blowin' baby."

"I'm whatever you want me to be as long as it gets you in that bed and me on the road," Donovan confirmed.

Donovan managed to get Reid to bed. Reid fell asleep as instantly as it took to see his bed. He slept all night without interruption, but woke up motion sick and in pain. Last night was a vague memory, but the sound of the train was as clear as quartz. "I can't believe that it happened two nights in a row." Reid mused. "Tonight then, I'll be ready."

Later that morning, Reid's mother came into the room. "Are you hungry? I made breakfast."

"I'll be right down, mom," Reid replied. She went downstairs and he closed his eyes, writhing in his nausea. He didn't feel like eating, but he also didn't want his mother to know he was suffering from a hangover. That was a conversation he didn't want to have.

Moments went by as Reid tried to get over the pain. He figured after a while that he was as good as he was going to get and went to the kitchen. "Reid, help your little brother into his high chair, will you?" His mother asked. Reid picked up the toddler and secured him into the chair. The toddler laughed and gripped Reid's hair.

"Ow, Eddie, let go of my hair please," Reid whispered as he pried the tiny fist away from his long black hair. Reid felt better after having breakfast. He told his mother he had a headache and she gave him some pain killers. Reid took Eddie to the living room with him while his mother went out to run errands. Eddie would get preoccupied watching his favorite shows and Reid sat on his favorite armchair. On the left arm of the couch, there was a small carving initial. Reid absent-mindedly ran his fingers along it.

When Reid was younger, he had a habit of carving his initials on things. Victims of this habit were the couch, his desk, the kitchen drawer and his dad's old toybox which was in Eddie's room. It was a nice feeling knowing that the initials were there. It was like letting the world know he had made a mark. He loved looking up to the night sky, but he could sometimes feel how small he was in comparison. It was comforting to know he left some sort of impact.

Reid's phone rang. He looked at the screen to see Donovan's name. He smiled and answered the phone. "Hey Donovan. Thanks for taking me home."

"No problem, just calling to make sure you were good. You really drank a lot last night."

"Yeah, I'm fine," Reid replied.

"Did miss Vasquez find out?" Donovan asked.

"No, mom didn't find out. Though I'm an adult, so I don't think she cares so much anymore."

"You were so drunk, man," Donovan chuckled. "You were swaying and mumbling and hearing things."

"The train whistle, right? I don't think I imagined that."

"Yeah, sure," Donovan said.

"No really," He persisted. "I heard the train the night before too and yes, I was sober. I think it's something else."

"Reid, there's not a train track around for miles of this town. It pretty much has to be something else."

Reid's mouth curled upward. "Do you wanna check it out tonight?"

"I'm not going out in the dead of night to look for a ghost train, are you serious?"

"Come on, Donovan. Remember when we were kids and we used to go out and explore? We used to sneak out at night and go to the cemetery or sneak around old buildings?"

"Yeah and in hindsight it's a miracle we didn't die," Donovan informed him. "Those abandoned buildings could have had some homeless crazy person or a gang or we could have gotten tetanus."

"I mean, we did meet a homeless man that one time," Reid reminded him.

"Yeah I remember and he brought us to our house because he was a responsible adult that knew two kids shouldn't be out in the middle of the night looking for ghosts."

"Well fine then, I'll go alone," Reid decided.

"Don't go alone," Donovan pleaded.

"You won't go with me so I'll have to go alone."

"If you die or disappear no one will know where you went."

"So does that mean you're coming with me?"

"Where's the 'don't go at all' option?" Donovan asked.

"There is no option like that," Reid said. "Either you come with me or I'm going alone."

"Why don't you ask someone else to go with you?" Donovan bargained.

"Because I already know no one else will go with me. They'd think I was crazy."

"I think you're crazy," Donovan countered.

"Yeah but you like that I'm crazy," Reid challenged.

"Whatever, shut up," Donovan muttered. "Fine I'm coming with you. What time do you want to meet up?"

The sun faded behind the horizon and darkness overtook the sky, leaving behind freckles of light which both overlooked the planet and had no knowledge of its existence. Two young men met on Reid's front porch, sitting in the chill and waiting for the haunting call of something that shouldn't exist.

"What do you think it is?" Reid asked.

"Hard to tell," Donovan replied. "I never heard it. How close do you think it is? Would we have to take the car?"

"I don't think so," Reid replied. "It sounds close. Like… When

I hear it, it sounds like it can't be more than a block away. It sounds... I can't describe it, it's like... It sounds like something you're afraid of but also you're excited about."

"Like a rollercoaster?" Donovan offered.

"Yeah! Oh, well... Almost. There's also a weird nostalgia to it. I don't know, it's just really nice. I wonder why you couldn't hear it."

Donovan shrugged, "I was a little preoccupied with getting you out of my car before you puked."

Reid fell silent, his eyes wide and his body still. Donovan opened his mouth, but Reid held up a hand. "Do you hear it?"

Donovan listened. He heard the whispering of the wind and the crackling of small rodents settling in the leaves. There were rumbling cars and whistling insects, but no matter how much he strained his ears, there was nothing remotely close to the sound of a train. "I'm sorry man, I don't hear it at all."

"What? How is that possible? It's so close." Reid patted Donovan's leg and stood up. "Come on, I'll lead. Let's go follow it."

"Wait, Reid, don't you think it's weird that you can listen to it and I can't?"

"Of course I think it's weird. That's why I want to see what it is. Are you not coming?"

Donovan sighed. "Yes, I'm coming."

Donovan stood up beside Reid and followed his friend into the shadows of the trees. He held the flashlight to the concrete path before them while Reid led the march closer to a sound which he had no reason to believe was anything other than imaginary. Reid picked up his pace, Donovan bounded quicker to shadow his friend. For a time, there were no words between them, only the padding of eager shoes and the desperate panting breaths.

"Are you sure we're going the right way," Donovan asked while he noticed how the houses gradually diminished and the trees gained recruits. He strained to keep up with Reid, who gave him no response. "Reid, can you hear me?" He cried. "Where are we going?!"

The train whistle called to Reid like a siren of the forest. While he was on this journey with his longest known friend, every sound, sight and sense were dulled by the increasing temptation of the mysterious whistle. He felt pressure to hurry on, as though he knew he would miss the train, but that feeling parented another feeling.

Reid was fully aware that he was losing control and that something was wrong. All time and reality faded from his conscious mind, which resulted in a dim, but present terror.

Donovan was losing his wind. Reid ran with seemingly no effort even though before he could barely run a block without panting. Donovan was losing ground. He tried to cry out to him to snap out of it. "Reid stop running! I have to catch my breath… Reid! Reid slow down!" Donovan went for one final push, using the last of his strength to launch himself towards his friend and grab at Reid's arm. "Got-…"

Donovan felt himself fall forward. Reid faded into the orchard. Donovan laid in the soft soil, panting, arms and legs rubbery, eyes wide and staring at the silhouettes of the branches stemming through the darkness lit only by the moon and stars. He knew his hand reached Reid's arm. He clearly grabbed at Reid's sweater sleeve, but there was no contact. Donovan's hand, to his confusion and mortification, had gone right through Reid's as though he were a ghost.

The whistling stopped. Reid slowed down his run. As sudden as a bee sting, Reid's entire body felt a rush of sudden burning aching pain. He gasped and stopped jogging at the sudden pain, resting his hands on his knees as he coughed and greedily inhaled as much air as he could. Where was he? He remembered following the mysterious train whistle with…

"Donovan?" Reid wheezed. He looked around for his friend but to his astonishment not only did he see no Donovan, but there were no trees, no road, no houses and no light. He stood heaving in the middle of a black abyss. Reid wanted to sit down and catch his breath, but he kept standing. Something wasn't right. He couldn't let himself get too comfortable. "Donovan!" He cried again. After he caught his breath, he turned the way he came and began walking when a burst of light bloomed from behind. Slowly, cautiously, Reid turned around.

Emanating the soft white glow, doors wide open, there waited a large, sighing train. "Oh," Reid cooed in awe. "There it is."

Reid had never seen a train up close before. There was something rustic, yet hauntingly beautiful about it. The train was pearly white. The smoke from the engineer's car roll and fell along the rest of the machine. If Reid didn't feel so much pain from the run he took, he would have thought he was dreaming. Reid walked closer to the train. He touched the side of the car that had the open door. He walked up the steps leading through the door. He walked into the train.

Reid felt something familiar. A wave of nostalgia hit him. Although he was positive that he had never ridden in a train before, something felt very familiar about the car he was in. In a sudden memory that almost made him chuckle, he thought of his dad. He thought of his dad's motorcycle. Reid walked further into the car, and the door closed behind him.

He should have been terrified. He knew that whatever was happening was likely something horrible and he may even lose his life.

Reid sat on the long, padded seat on the side of the car. Everything was so quiet. He wasn't sure if he could even make a sound. He had a strange feeling that his voice wouldn't come out.

"What is this place?" He asked out loud mostly to test his theory. Even as he was able to speak, the words halted in the air without echo or response. Reid closed his eyes and rested his head against the train. The train sighed in response. Reid felt his body jerk and tilt to the left. The sigh of the train became a pattern of decisive chugs. Reid couldn't keep his eyes open.

"You seem quite comfortable."

Reid slowly opened his eyes. Standing before him was a pale man wearing a pinstripe suit. Reid lifted his eyes to see that the man had no face, only a bright, gray smile. Reid knew somewhere in his mind that under normal circumstances, he would be screaming. This being before him was outright monstrous, like jagged lines in a soft portrait. In the way Reid was right then, however, he couldn't manage a single cry of surprise. "Who are you," Reid demanded sleepily.

"Jazzer's the name, and this is my domain," The creature replied. Jazzer twirled his cane and tipped his hat before Reid. "I don't recall expecting any passengers. Do you have your ticket?"

"Ticket?" Reid whispered. He rubbed his eyes and sat up a bit more. "I was hearing this noise," He tried to explain.

"Yes, very good," Jazzer interrupted. "No matter. This train has two destinations. One way is your destination," He held out a hand. "The other is not your destination," He held out the other.

"How do I know which is which?" Reid asked.

A deep, amused chuckle escaped Jazzer's grinning maw. "My

you are an interesting one. You remind me of a passenger I had several years ago. If I was a gambling man, and I happen to be, I would bet you know that passenger. He went by the name Diego back then."

Reid's eyes widened. He struggled to stay awake. "Diego Vasquez? That's my dad."

Jazzer put a finger to his chin. "Ha, yes, that was the very one."

"My dad," Reid strained to say. "Disappeared fifteen years ago."

"I have never known anything to disappear," Jazzer revealed. "Only relocate."

Reid's eyes closed. His body was heavy and it was nearly impossible to speak. "Where is he?"

"Who?" Jazzer asked.

"Diego Vasquez," Reid clarified.

"Which one?" Jazzer grinned wider.

"Please," Reid whispered. "What do I have to do?"

Reid opened his eyes to find that he was alone in the cart. He scanned around looking for anything, but found only an empty cart. Reid yawned and rubbed at his face again. He had to stay awake. He was in danger. His father could be here somewhere.

"Come on," He scolded himself. "Just get up. Why is it so hard?" Reid thought about his mother who would be worried about him and his brother that he wanted to see grow up. Reid thought of his friends. He thought about Donovan who was probably freaking out about Reid disappearing. He had to stay awake and find a way off this train. He felt like an idiot. This was such a stupid idea. Why was it so important for him to find the noise anyway?

Reid tilted his head to look out the window. The scene took his breath away. Where the stars before seemed to be a passive observer, through the train window he could see them dancing. The distant beacons hopped and floated around each other, never leaving their general position but communicating with silent sways and skips. Reid witnessed them with a content smirk. The twinkling dancers lulled Reid back to sleep.

A distant buzzing sound caused Reid to stir. The buzzing got louder and more obnoxious. It was jarring, but familiar. Reflexively, he swung his arm across his body.

The noise stopped once his hand hit the snooze button. Reid rubbed at his eyes and blinked a few times, allowing his eyes to adjust to the light and colors. He was snug in covers, the rising sun beaming through the curtains of his window from his own room.

"Wait," Reid shot out of bed. "No. This isn't right."

Reid rushed out to the kitchen where he saw his mother cooking breakfast. "Oh Reid," She chimed. "I was about to come get you to have breakfast. Help your little brother into his high chair, will you?"

"Yeah," Reid blinked. "Sure thing." Reid picked up his brother and the toddler reciprocated with a giggle and a fist in Reid's hair."

"Ow, Eddie, let go of my hair, please…" Reid pried Eddie's hand away and put him into the high chair. Reid froze. "Huh, weird."

Mrs. Vasquez turned to her oldest. "What's weird?"

"I had the strangest feeling of Déjà vu," Reid admitted. "Mom, what day is it?"

Mrs. Vasquez put the back of her hand to Reid's forehead. "Are you feeling alright, Reid?"

"No, I mean, yeah I'm alright," Reid lied. "Just a headache, I guess."

"I'll get you some pain medication," Mrs. Vasquez offered as she rifled through the junk drawer for the pills.

Reid took the pills silently. Everything felt too surreal, as though he had done all this before. He remembered that he had a crazy dream last night, but he couldn't remember what it was about.

"Reid, after breakfast do you mind watching your brother while I go out to run some errands?"

"No problem, mom," Reid replied. He decided that he just needed some time to wake up.

Reid took Eddie to the living room with him while his mother went out to run errands. Eddie would get preoccupied watching his favorite shows and Reid sat on his favorite armchair. Reid absent-mindedly ran his fingers along the left arm of the couch.

"What," Reid whispered. He explored the entire wooden surface of the couch. When he couldn't feel it, he took a closer look at the armrest. It was gone.

"Is this a new couch?" He thought to himself. But no, this was the same worn blue armchair with the same unsightly stains. Every tear and thread of the couch was the same, except…

"What happened to my initials?" Reid asked nobody in

particular. He ran his finger along the wood once again to feel any sort of trace, but it was as initial-less as the rest of the couch. There was no scratch-out, no repair, no evidence at all.

Reid sprung into the kitchen. He went to the kitchen drawer hung up to the left of the fridge. On the lower left corner where his initials were before now hung there untouched by any carving. "What the heck is going on here?!" Reid rushed up the stairs to his room. Maybe it was a new couch and a new dresser, but his desk would be unmistakable. Reid saw the same clutter of papers, the same laptop, the same stains and the same old stickers he used to stick on the side. Reid sat on the chair and scooted in. He felt under the desk, beneath the pull-out keyboard shelf. It was as smooth as new.

Reid's breathing quickened. He threatened to hyperventilate. The only initial left to check was Eddie's room where his dad's old toybox was left.

Something itched the back of his mind like a distant memory. He strained to remember his dream. He thought for some reason it had something to do with looking for his dad.

Reid paced himself to Eddie's room. Reid tiptoed around Eddie's toy jungle to the near empty toybox. On the lid of the box, it read 'Diego' in familiar cursive letters. Reid smiled lightly and traced his fingers on the carving. He lifted the lid. As expected, and also to his surprise, the cursive 'RV' that he remembered carving on the wood more clearly than he could remember his own name was absent from the deep redwood toybox. It was like he was never there. Without knowing what else to do, Reid called Donovan. When he didn't answer, he called again, and then again.

"Donovan," He cried out when he finally answered. Reid gripped his phone so close to him that his voice was muffled.

"Reid, what's the deal, man?" Donovan asked. "You keep calling but you know I'm at work."

"Donovan, something has happened. All of my initials are gone."

"All of your what?" Donovan asked.

"My initials, you know," Reid replied incredulously. "You were there when I did most of them. Remember? I carved my initials on the couch and on my dad's toybox?"

"Um," Donovan fell silent for a few seconds. "Sorry man, I don't remember that."

"Donovan I'm freaking out," Reid admitted. "If you're joking around stop it. I woke up and just something is very wrong."

"Are you still drunk?" Donovan asked.

"What?"

"You were completely wasted last night," Donovan explained. "You were slurring and talking about a train and stumbling around. You didn't get alcohol poisoning or something, did you?"

"Wait, what's that about a train noise?"

"You were talking about hearing a train even though there's nothing like that anywhere around here."

"Donovan," Reid breathed. "You have to help me find that train again tonight."

"Again? What do you mean? You know what, never mind. Reid, I gotta get back to work. I'll call you after work, alright?"

Donovan drove to Reid's house later that night. Reid sat on the front porch, waiting. Donovan got out of his car to go sit with his oldest friend. Reid was eerily quiet. Donovan was almost afraid to break the silence. "Reid. What's wrong?"

"I don't really know," Reid hung his head. "I know something is wrong though. Something happened to me last night. I can hardly remember…"

The sun retreated behind the planet, taking its light and leaving only specks of itself. Donovan spied on Reid's profile. He had never seen Reid so serious before. Donovan opened his mouth to say something when Reid stood from his spot. Without another word, he started walking. "Wait, Reid. Where are you going?" Donovan asked.

"It was right around this time. I'm going to find the train."

"What train? Hey, Reid, going out late at night like this is dangerous."

Reid made a half-turn towards Donovan. "You don't have to come." Leaving his friend paralyzed with confusion, Reid turned to walk down the driveway and towards the orchard.

"Reid," Donovan called out with no response. Donovan got up and hurried to keep pace with him. "Reid you're scaring me," He admitted.

Reid heard no whistle. All he had were vague memories carrying his way towards the orchard. He was using every bit of his attention to remember. He remembered following the noise. He remembered the orchard. He just had to keep going. Not far from here there was… Just a little further he would find…

Memories of his father came rushing back. He remembered he was very young when the police came to his mother to report that there were no leads or evidence. He remembered when the case went cold. He remembered the late-night drives on his dad's motorcycle. He remembered when his mother was forced to sell the motorcycle. He remembered how his mother tried to move on. He remembered how he tried to move on. Before his mother met someone else and had Eddie, it was just him and mother after his father disappeared.

Not disappeared. Relocated.

"Reid, stop!"

A rough pull back on the sleeve of his sweater jarred Reid back to the present. He turned to see Donovan, panting, eyes wide. Reid was breathing heavily too. His sides hurt. How long had he been running?

"Come on Reid, you have to stop. You're going to hit the river at this rate."

"The river?" Reid panted. He looked back to where he was heading. That's right, he remembered now. The river behind the orchard had a current too strong to cross. The river had always been there. He looked back to Donovan. "I'm sorry."

Donovan hung his head and tried to catch his breath. "It's alright, man. Hey listen, let's just go back to your place, play some video games, and forget this ever happened."

Reid's chest and shoulders heaved. He closed his eyes. "Alright," He conceded.

In the days that passed, Reid re-carved all his old places. He never heard the train whistle again, and everything else was exactly as it was. It was as though nothing really did happen after all.

THE LUCKIEST MAN

There was a man in the village who was incredibly lucky. He didn't think much about it, but the villagers around him were filled with envy. Whenever something happened to him, villagers would always muse. Heppni was the handsomest. Heppni never had any trouble. He would always find the money he needed. He would always find the company he wanted. Heppni always found the largest game when the villagers hunted. Heppni's home was always the warmest and comfiest. Even with all of this good fortune, he never took it for granted. Whenever he saw a hungry man, Heppni shared his food. Whenever Heppni found more wealth than he needed, he would share it with his neighbors. "Why are we not as lucky as you," His friends would lament. "I would share my luck if I could," Heppni responded. "In the meantime, please accept what I can give."

The day came where the village chief's daughter was old enough to wed. The chief wanted her to marry another leader from another village, but no villages had any eligible suitor. "How can I expand the village," The chief grieved. "If there is no one who can have my daughter?" As he lamented, his daughter asked, "Father, can I marry someone from the village?"

"Who did you have in mind," The chief asked. The young woman blushed and twisted her finger in her hair.

"There is a man who is the luckiest man in the village. He is fairly wealthy and shares his good fortune selflessly. He is very handsome and he would treat me with respect."

"Are you speaking of Heppni," The chief inquired. He thought for a moment. If the rumors about Heppni were true, then perhaps the boy would project his good luck on the village and on his daughter if they were wed. "Very well, it will be done."

News traveled to the farthest stretch of the village. In a matter of hours, everyone knew of Heppni's engagement to the chief's daughter.

A small group of men grew angry with this news. "Why must this man be blessed with so many fine things? He never has to work for all of his fortune and now he will live as a leader of our village," They claimed. "Surely, Heppni's luck must soon run out," They thought.

In their frustration, they formulated a plan. The night before the ceremony, they invited Heppni for a drink to celebrate. Once Heppni celebrated so much that he could no longer walk, the men held him down. They cut open his beautiful face. They stuffed him into a burlap sack and tied him in. They also tied a rope around his neck to strangle him quietly. Once Heppni no longer moved or cried, they sliced his stomach open and threw him into the forest for the animals to eat. The men congratulated each other, relieved that they rid him from the village.

That night, a pack of starving rats followed the scent of fresh meat to the village. They ate at the meat, but they were unsatisfied. As luck would have it, the men that murdered Heppni slept together in a hut close to the forest. The rats they attracted headed towards the hut to get shelter from the cold. Unluckily, every person in the hut woke up terribly ill. Luckily, no one ese in the hut caught the disease. The infected bled from their noses and mouths. They wretched and their hands and feet blackened. Within a week only one was left alive. He claimed all this was punishment for murdering Heppni. He told the villagers where to find the body and begged for Heppni to release him from this torture. He perished the following day.

The frightened and grieving villagers found Heppni's remains. They buried him in the center of the village. After that day, Every time the village had good fortune, Heppni's old friends would fondly claim it was him finally sharing his luck as he always hoped to do, and they knew to never turn Heppni away.

THE FOREST WITCH

Deep in the forests of an old island, far from the clutches of humanity, where the beasts rest and the yokai play, there lived an old witch. The villagers called her an old spirit of the forest. They said that they could hear her cackle as the wind whistled through the branches. Some villagers believed that she lured children into the forest to eat them while others believed that she was an ancient guardian of the forest. Perhaps both were true. Aiko never thought she would ever go into the forest. Of all the villagers that lived in Hoshi, she was the most cowardly. She feared the forest and everything in it, especially the fabled witch, Baba. Aiko's eyes glistened with tears, her body trembling as she gripped a basket of treats so tightly that her knuckles went white. The newborn day lit her way to the forest, but as though the light itself felt hesitant, it only touched the first few trees.

Aiko whimpered, but compelled her foot to step forward. She heard the birds singing. They were urging her on, she thought, or warning her away. Aiko took a deep breath and another step.

With every move forward, she was certain that she would faint. Only the thought of her task and her desperation kept her legs from buckling under her weight. Aiko took in a staggered breath. "Baba," She squeaked. The bush beside her feet rustled. She screamed and jumped in the air as a small furry creature darted out of the bush. She almost dropped the basket, but held onto it desperately as she breathed to calm her heart. She could still see the village. She could turn back. Aiko whimpered and wiped away her tears. She shakily took a few more steps. "Baba," She wailed a bit louder.

There was a low growl. The young woman cried out and her body turned her around to run, but she scolded herself and remained still. She observed the trees and the sounds. She heard the growling again. It came from her left, so she stepped silently towards the right. She looked back to the village, the sight of it giving her courage. It was right there. She would be alright.

As she turned away, the wind cackled, freezing Aiko's spine. She spun around to find that the village was no longer in sight. She turned around again. Nothing looked familiar. As far as she could tell, she was in the center of the forest. She tried to walk back, just so she could see Hoshi and gather her bearings, but there was no end to the forest. Aiko sank to her knees, basket cradled tightly in her arms. Her breathing stuttered, her body chilled, she called out as loudly as possible. "Baba!"

Without the sight of her village to soothe her, she lost all willpower to go on. She heaved and frantically tried to think of what to do. Her mind grasped for a motive and thought about her sick son, bedridden and dying. That's right, if she didn't have the sight of the village to urge her to keep going, she would remind herself of her child to urge her to not give up.

With unsteady legs, Aiko pushed forward. She heard distant calls of creatures she never heard before. She heard branches falling from trees and twigs cracking under the weight of the invisible life around her. Anything could kill her, but she couldn't give up. She would never give up. Not until her son was healed. Baba was her son's last hope.

The wind cackled again. Aiko turned to see a small cottage in a clearing that wasn't there before. Relieved for a sign of life, she hurried to the front door of the little home. After looking back to make sure nothing was following her, she knocked on the door.

"Please," She begged. "My child is sick. I need your help."

"Eeehehehehe," An old woman stood behind Aiko. The smiling crone shuffled closer to the shivering young woman. "What is that in your arms?" Baba asked.

Aiko slowly held the basket to Baba. She wanted to throw the basket at Baba and run, but the memory of her bedridden son kept her feet planted on the witch's front step. "A gift," She forced her words to let go of her tongue. "As an offering to you, to consider helping me save my son."

"Hmmm?" Baba raised her head up to the fair young woman, tired eyes hidden behind wrinkles studying her face. "How do you know that I won't eat your son instead?"

Aiko felt all the air leave from her body. Baba cackled again.

"Come in and have some tea," She offered. Baba waved her hand and the door to the cottage swung open. Baba shuffled into the cottage. Aiko waited for the old woman to walk inside before she struggled to take off her shoes and follow suit. "Set the basket onto the kotatsu," Baba instructed. Aiko did as she was told. She looked around the cottage, carvings of various yokai and plants decorated the beams. Everything looked hundreds of years old, including the cottage. "Have a seat," Baba said, and with a start Aiko followed her orders once more, tucking her legs beneath her.

Aiko watched Baba inch her way to a red tea kettle and tea set. The cups were uneven and the kettle bumpy, as though they were sculpted by a child. The old woman set two cups down and shakily lifted the kettle of tea to each cup. "Now," Baba set the kettle down. "You have come to my forest alone. Why?"

Aiko bowed her head. "Forgive me, if I told anyone what I was going to do, my husband would have forbidden it."

"The forest is a dangerous place for any human," Baba's voice went graver.

Aiko couldn't look Baba in the eye and instead kept her head bowed. "Yes," She confirmed softly.

"What is wrong with your son?" Baba asked.

Her voice caught in her throat a moment. "Nobody knows," Aiko raised her head lightly, her cheeks wet. "He has a fever. He cannot eat or speak and he cannot walk. My husband and I have tried to speak to every doctor and no one can give us an answer."

Baba took a sip of her tea and opened the basket. Fresh onigiri waited inside. Baba took one out and took a bite. "You are a very brave young woman to seek a witch in this forest alone. You are also very kind to bring me a gift." Baba unsteadily stood from her seat and wandered back to her counter. She took a small wooden tea container. Carved on the lid was the image of a phoenix. Baba sat back down at the kotatsu and handed her the container. "This tea will cure your son. Make him drink a cup of this once in the morning and once at night. In two weeks, he will be healthier than anyone in the village."

Aiko took the container as though it were made of porcelain. She gazed down at it, quivering fingers tracing the phoenix. "Baba, thank you," She whispered.

"I merely offered you the prize," Baba cackled. "It is you, Aiko, that took the journey."

Aiko turned her head to ask Baba how she knew her name, but was shocked to see only the forest. Aiko looked around her. She sat before the forest in the midafternoon, birds chirping to welcome her back. Aiko stood up quickly, tea container in hand, and turned back to her village. Behind her, as she made her way home, she could hear the wind cackling through the trees.

CHASE

The sun shone warmly against Reginald's face. He knew a delightful morning was to behold him as he wandered to his front door to collect the newspaper. Reginald loved to read up on current events. While outside, he noticed a familiar figure walking up from the sidewalk. "Maggie, my dear!" He called to her. She laughed her usual chiming laugh. "Reginald, I had hoped you would be up and about. How are you dear friend?"

Reginald held the door open for her. "Good, good," He replied. "I would have thought you'd be here with Wiggy."

Maggie waved him off. "Oh, you know Wiggy. That charming eccentric! You can never keep track of that boy."

"Oh, I think I see him now," Reginald pointed towards the other side of the street where a red-headed man came bounding up. He called out to the approaching man, "Wiggy! How are you doing, darling boy?!"

Wiggy hopped up the porch and followed inside with the others. "Doing rather well, Reggie!" He smiled. "I see that Maggie has beat me here."

Maggie laughed, "Did you try to take one of your shortcuts again? I keep telling you they aren't as short of a trip as you think."

"Broken."

"What was that, Wiggy?" Reginald turned to his friend. Wiggy only shrugged and shook his head. "I said nothing, friend."

"Broken."

Reginald turned to Maggie who also seemed unaware. Almost instantly, Reginald forgot as well. "Care for some tea?" He asked his friends as he turned to the kitchen. But there was no kitchen, only a white wall.

"Wakey wakey Chase, time to start the day!"

"Where are they?" A quieter voice asked the white wall. The voice startled Reggie since it wasn't his voice and yet he felt it coming from his own throat.

"There is no 'they,' Chase. Just you and me."

Chase spun to the other side of his body. He was lying down, surrounded by white walls. A shadow blocked the door.

"Go away. I don't want you here!" Chase sat up from the cot and held his arms up against his face. The shadows. They always come. Why won't they leave him alone?!

"Come on you big baby, we have to eat breakfast and get you ready for the day. We're having eggs, sausage and pancakes today. All your favorites."

Wait, that voice. That was no shadow. In fact, it sounded like Wiggy. He was being summoned for breakfast, and honestly Reginald was famished. "May I have some coffee with breakfast?"

"Sure, why not?"

Reginald stepped out of bed and was about to meet Wiggy on the other side of the room when he noticed that his floor had a large hole down to the first floor. Who could have done this? 'Most likely the shadows,' Reginald thought with disdain. What monstrous demons they were. "Wiggy, I'll be jumping to you. Be prepared to catch me!" Reginald cried as he took an impressive flying leap towards his friend.

"You made it, good job!" Wiggy cried as he gripped his friend's hand to keep him from falling down. Reginald chuckled. "I still have a spring in my leap even after all these years."

Reginald was familiar with the community of the apartment. He spent many nights visiting Wiggy there. He enjoyed the art hung on the walls and though the tenants were generally quite odd, Reginald often enjoyed their company in passing. He bowed his head lightly to those he passed. Some wouldn't acknowledge him but others would at least smile back and wave.

On the way down to the community kitchen, Reginald looked to a window to see the blooming flowers. What he witnessed instead was Wiggy. It was the form of his friend though much younger, staring at him, mouth agape, eyes white, skin blackening into a void as though he were being swallowed by the abyss of the black unknown. Seeing this sick trick that the shadows were playing on him, he wondered how he would bring it up to Wiggy. His friend seemed to notice Reginald staring at something since he called for his attention. "Chase, just ignore it. Come on, we have to get you to eat."

"But," Reginald began, though as he met Wiggy's worried gaze Reginald decided to keep the shadow's vision silent for now.

They were seated at the kitchen table with their breakfast at last. Wiggy set down their coffee and Reginald took a few moments to blow on the hot liquid, taking in the aroma. Upon his first sip, Reginald was taken aback. "My Wiggy, this coffee is magnificent."

"Why thank you," Wiggy replied.

"I simply must know where you get your beans, dear boy."

"Cambodia, as a matter of fact," Wiggy smiled. Reginald knew that Wiggy was proud of his coffee business, so offered any praise he could to support his lifelong friend.

"Cambodia you say, how delightful!"

Breakfast with Wiggy was as grand as ever, even as the shadows darted and loomed around them, Wiggy was always a welcoming sight. He came to Reginald every morning. Every morning? Surely. Reginald couldn't think of a morning without him.

"My, there are a lot of birds outside today." Maggie poured herself a warm cup of chamomile tea as they rested on the porch of Reginald's white-fenced home.

"Yes, they must be returning from the South," Wiggy responded. "Birds tend to fly where it is warmest."

"How do you suppose they know when it's time to fly?" Maggie wondered. "Even after the first cold, some birds remain. I don't think all birds do travel South for the winter."

"Of course they do, Maggie," Wiggy explained. "Perhaps it is only that some birds fly later than others."

"I've seen birds even in the coldest of winter," Maggie claimed. "Reginald, you've seen them too, haven't you?"

Wiggy and Maggie turned to Reginald, who smiled, "Perhaps there are some birds that stay to withstand the weather. Either that or they somehow get left behind."

"Hmph," Wiggy replied, taking a drink. "I suppose that is a possibility." Wiggy looked down to his cup. "Reginald ol' bean, do you have any coffee? I'm afraid I just do not have the heart for something so sweet this evening."

"Coffee?" Maggie's face soured. "In my opinion, this tea isn't sweet enough."

"Well Wiggy, it just so happens," Reginald admitted. "There is a fine young man who lives right around the corner. Would you like more cream?" He added to Maggie. She silently offered her cup to him, so he may add to her tea while he continued to speak. "He has a father with a coffee bean business and he sent his dear son over to bring me some," he continued.

Maggie placed the tips of her fingers to her chest. "I'm sure he's a fine young man, but I'm afraid I shall pass. Chamomile is the only thing I will drink."

"Haha, oh Maggie, you and your tea," Reginald chuckled.

"What was the name of the boy who brought you the beans?" The question sounded like it came from Wiggy, yet as soon as it was asked, it was forgotten.

Reginald closed his eyes and hummed a tune. It was a sweet, catchy tune that would always get stuck in his head. Wiggie and Maggie fell silent to listen. They were all fond of the song. Maggie took a long sip of her tea. "I am so delighted by that melody," She mused. "I do wish it had a title."

"Reggie ol' bean," Wiggy interrupted. "Have you been doing well?"

Reginald halted his humming to reply, "Ah, oh yes. I have been doing quite fine. My roses are growing quite beautifully, and I managed to fix that darn washing machine."

"Oh? Who broke the washing machine?" Maggie asked, but as soon as it was asked, it was forgotten.

Reginald heard a click and metal sliding against metal.

"Go away! Can't you see I'm in the middle of having coffee?!" He addressed the foreign noise. Even as he spoke, the scene darkened. To Reginald's surprise and dismay, the faces of his friends as well as the porch, the birds and everything else melted like a heated oil painting. The colors and shapes merged and left only black tar and disfigured visions.

Reginald heard a faint voice in the darkness, a low murmur dragging him, beckoning him into the tar and the madness.

"No, what have you done?!" He cried to the ever-growing sound of some devil approaching him.

"It's time for your medicine Chase," The looming voice warned.

Who was Chase? Reginald was unfamiliar. He turned to see a red image with flaming hair looming closer to him. The hair reminded him of the younger Wiggy he watched through the window. Was this the same shadow? Memories came of this monster, the bringer of the darkness, the master of the shadows. Overcome with terror, Reginald tried to push away.

"Aah! No, stay away!" Reginald ran from the portal which the creature came only to hit a soft barrier. He tried to push it back. He tried to run from the tar demons and their fire-headed master.

"No! What was that?!" Chester darted his eyes to the sky to find to his horror that the tar had blocked out the sky and was now oozing its residue all over the ground. The tar demons crawled and slithered closer, all of them staring at him. "Who are these people?!" He demanded.

"Please Chase, we have all come to play." The fire-haired demon grew larger and larger, grinning its inhuman smile, eyes deep and blue enough to drown in. Drowning. Reginald found him suffocating. Reginald was drowning.

"Back away!" Reginald gasped. The demon paid him no heed. Its claws burned his skin. Its snarl an unwelcome final image for Reginald as he began to fade. Images flashed into his mind, not of him, but of another man. A young boy, a broken washing machine, a broken door, broken screams, broken home, broken spirits, broken. Broken.

Shattered glass shards surrounded him, reflecting different faces. Shadows, monsters, Reginald. Chase. Wiggy. Maggie. He saw the fire demon, he saw the tar demons, he saw the younger Wiggy's face again, fading into blackness. These shards, they were fragments of memories. They were bits and pieces of a puzzle. Fear became curiosity. It was at that moment he realized he didn't know who he was. Reginald, of course. But no. Reginald drowned. There was another person lost in the sea of broken things.

The shattered glass became a single mirror. The face in the mirror belonged to a small black-haired boy with porcelain-blue eyes, simple enough to shatter. He looked around. He was in a bathroom.

The young boy took a moment to view his surroundings. There was a door. He opened it. Inside was a long hallway, portraits covering every portion of the wall that was not a light or another door.

He stepped soundlessly through the hallway. Lights flickered at the other end. Candles whispered in the large room. Chairs pushed back from the center of the room where candles lay. They rest in a circle on the ground, surrounded by a pattern in chalk. The soft flickering rose, as did fingers from the darkness. Then came the arms, and then the eyes. What also rose came the voices, whispers invading his mind and disorienting his thoughts. He had to run, to leave the noise, to leave the shadows. The boy turned and ran back towards the bathroom, but the hallway stretched, more and more portraits hung down, their attention constantly upon the fleeing child. His weight increased, gravity bidding the boy to slow, then crawl, then drag. The voices grew deafeningly loud, an undertone of organs and violins grew to a crescendo. The boy's ears would soon go deaf if this continued. He tried to scream, but his lungs were as heavy as his body. Then suddenly...

"Pop!" Like the bursting of a balloon, everything became weightless and silent.

"Buddy, it's just me."

That voice breathed life back into Reginald. He searched among the darkness to see his dear old friend. "Wiggy, ol' bean, what are you doing in a place like this?"

"It's breakfast time," Reginald heard Wiggy say. "Hurry up before it gets cold. If you want, you can even have some more of that coffee you like so much."

"O-oh, of course," Reginald unsteadily made his way to Wiggy and took the man's hand. "That sounds delightful Wiggy, thank you."

Breakfast was, as expected, wonderful. He had a decent conversation with Wiggy about the quality of coffee. From Cambodia, how exotic! "I believe it would be well to visit the neighbors," Reginald decided. There was a park nearby which many from the neighborhood frequented. This was a pleasant place for the most part. Some of his neighbors weren't very talkative, and some were downright uncivil, but Reginald had a few friendly faces he looked forward to see. Lily spoke of her grand kids that would visit her. Maisy was a nurse in the war and had epic stories so long as nobody mentioned blood. Henry and his talking monkey named Wooly always had the nicest things to say and they always spoke with such calm, relaxing voices.

After a delightful picnic lunch with Henry and Wooly, Wiggy approached them with a somber look. "Chase," He called to him. "Yes, Wiggy?" Reginald asked. He excused himself, apologizing to Henry and Wooly. He needed to be there for his best friend, and he certainly seemed uneasy.

"There is someone here to meet you," Wiggy admitted. A guest at his house? It couldn't have been Maggie, not with the look Wiggy was giving him. Someone to meet him? The world began to mute as Wiggy led him through hallways so strange and yet familiar. His movements remembered this path, and Reginald began to have this terrified, sinking feeling. But Wiggy would never lead him to danger. No, never Wiggy.

The room was not in Wiggy's apartment, nor was it at Reginald's house. This was... The in-between room. That was what he called it because it was like a room of memories, both his and not his, good and bad. This was the room of shattered pieces. He saw the face and slowly the room became darker. Tears clogged his airway and he was drowning again. The in-between room was giving him a very bad memory.

"Hello Chase. Can you hear me?" She asked him.

Reginald continued to drown again. Further and further down he went, and Chase began to wake up. He tried to warn Wiggy of this demon, but as his eyes darted towards Wiggy, there instead was a man Chase only barely recognized. Chase couldn't understand what they were talking about, but the more he looked to the woman the more he began to remember. The broken pieces began to come together.

"Devils are within him, don't you see?"

She said that before. In the room with the candles. He remembered his arms and legs were bound. He remembered being in the center of the circle. Devils. Chase saw something. He knew something he wasn't supposed to know. The woman was quite loud, wasn't she? 'You idiot,' 'You imbecile.' Stinging. Burning. Pain. Shame. The candles caused visions to ebb and flow before him.

Poor Chase, Reginald thought. Surely what happened to him would surely not happen to someone like Reginald. Reginald was a composed and respected member of society. Chase broke things he didn't know he broke. Chase would get beaten for his fits. Chase's father caught him witnessing his father be very friendly with his brother's female friends. Chase's mother caught him witnessing her having meetings with men in red robes speaking in unknown languages and reading books with strange languages. No one listened to Chase, and they shouldn't. Chase was a whiny child always seeing things. No one listened, so Chase wouldn't speak. Not to worry, his mother would beat the demons out of him. She dragged him into the bathroom, touching him, cleansing him. He remembered one of the red robes, he- No, he didn't want to think about that. No, not these memories, not again. Get out, Chase pleaded. Wake up Reginald, Chase cried.

There was a click and a creak. Chase's eyes darted to the door. Wiggy, he… He was gone. But the woman was still there. Chase noticed a man that peeked through the doorway, nodded at the woman, then closed the door. Chase recognized the man, he looked different out of the red robe. Chase spun his head back to the woman. Alone. Chase was alone with the woman.

"Finally," The woman's two black empty sockets faced the boy. "Don't worry. We will cleanse you at last."

The chair toppled underneath the boy as he pressed his back against the wall. Shadows emerged from her feet, stretching, moaning, grabbing at the boy. "Leave me alone," He begged. "If you hurt me, Wiggy won't like it."

"Just stay still, Chase," The devil woman replied. She pulled out a vial, and it was glowing. The woman's red eyes fixed upon him. "If you drink this, you will be cleansed. We can be happy again, the whole family."

"Don't touch me," The boy screamed. She came closer, her grip more powerful than that of the fire demon. She was going to break his arm. She squeezed his face hard, prying open his mouth. She poured the glowing clear liquid down his throat. He was drowning, drowning. Dying. Dying. Everything went black.

He had no idea how much time had passed. He felt… Taller than he remembered. Chase continued to see only darkness. What little light came to him revealed only blurs of color. He was in a bed, that much he knew. As his vision cleared, he saw padded walls. He saw a bed chained to the floor. He saw rags, certainly not the sort of finery Reginald would be seen wearing. This wasn't Reginald. It was Chase. But Chase was dead, he thought.

Chase wanted to call out to Wiggy, to ask why he left him all alone, but his voice was raspy, and he could barely speak without coughing. He tried to call out to Maggie, but there was the same reaction.

Loneliness.

Lonely like the room with the candles. Lonely like the feeling of not being heard, not being believed. Lonely like the sad, broken boy with no friends. Reginald. Where was Reginald?

"There is a fine young man who lives right around the corner. Would you like more cream?"

Chase repeated these words from memory. Like Reginald… Like in the radio show. No. Reginald was real, Wiggy and Maggie were… "He has a father with a coffee bean business and he sent his dear son over to bring me some," he continued.

The wall he stared at did not budge. The shadows, however, they continued to surround him, but this time, there was no Wiggy, no Maggie, no Reginald to keep them at bay.

"Haha, oh Maggie, you and your tea."

His eyes hot, body trembling, shadows wrapping around his throat, memories becoming more and more vivid. 'You broke it,' The shrill voice of the devil woman became a roar in his ears.

'You always break everything, you idiot! Go to the bathroom to face your punishment. Stop squirming! You broke the washing machine! I should lock you in and start it up. Wait until your father gets home. He'll kill you, you know. It's a good thing you have me to keep him at bay. We must starve the demons in you.' Vivid visions and sounds of water filling his head. The shadows choked him. He couldn't breathe. Flashes of himself looking through the mirror and a younger Wiggy blinked back and forth into his mind. Both scared, both drowning. 'Save him!' Drowning. 'Save him!' Drowning. Nothing to stop it. Nowhere to go. All alone. Broken. Broken.

Humming.

Somewhere in the white noise, there was humming.

He knew that song. It was a gentle, slow, soft melody. He couldn't remember the name, but he knew the tune. He began to hum with it.

For a few moments, all he could do was hum with the song. He kept his eyes closed. The shadows kept dancing around, yet for some reason he felt like they couldn't reach him. He was still terrified. He was in mourning. Wiggy and Maggie were dead for good. Reginald was dead for good. He had no idea who he was or where he was, but in the ethereal void of dancing shadows and uncertainty, there was a song. The song felt like the warm Sun. It felt like the gentle breeze, the feeling of laughing, the security of a simple, mundane past. Slowly, the song no longer became humming but rather the sound of a music box, strumming the same melody. His vision caught small glimpses of the box beyond the flailing demons. White porcelain ensnared by black veins floated just beyond his reach, and over time it was all he could see, as though it cast away the shadows, and for a brief moment he was no longer afraid.

The music box and the song snapped out of existence and white was all he could see. White, and a yellow lighting behind him. A shadow lay beside him. It was his shadow.

"Chase," He heard Wiggy's voice call. No, Wiggy was dead. The voice was graver, more lifeless. He turned his body around to see who it was. The man looked a lot like Wiggy, except he wasn't. The impersonator was calling him. Chase was his name, wasn't it? Chase sat up in bed. Was he always in bed? How long had he been asleep?

It came to a point where he couldn't look at the man anymore. Chase's eyes trailed down. That was when the memories came back. At last, without Wiggy, without Maggie, the shadows got him. He closed his eyes and began to sob.

"Help me, please," He whispered through sobs. "I can't see them."

"Isn't that a good thing?" The indifferent, ghost of Wiggy's voice replied.

"You don't understand."

"Chase, I'm sorry for what happened yesterday. How do you feel? Any pain?" The boy known as Chase shook his head. He wasn't sure if it was true.

"That's good. I can see you're not ready to go eat yet. So how about I come back after a little while, and I can see if I can't bring breakfast to you. How does that sound?"

"Okay."

He was alone again. Chase. He didn't want to be Chase, but since Reginald was dead he had no other choice. The shadows were out of sight but he could still hear them talk in his head. He was Chase. He was alone. He was locked up for what Chase did. Chase was locked up for what he did.

"I brought coffee." The voice startled him. It was the man again, the one that kept looking less and less like Wiggy.

"Can I sit on the bed with you?" The stranger asked. Chase did not protest. He found comfort in the stranger. His presence was as soothing as a lullaby.

"Chase, do you know who I am?"

Wiggy was Reginald's friend, but who was Wiggy to Chase? In the avalanche of upsetting memories, Chase thought hard about the answer. He looked away, trying to remember. If Wiggy was dead, then who else did Chase know? "I don't think so."

"You call me Wiggy."

The stranger knew Wiggy. "I can't see him anymore," He admitted.

"Do you know Eloise?"

The song? Yes, that was the name of the song in the music box. Chase hummed a few bars, hoping the stranger would join, but he did not. Why would the stranger ask about the song if he didn't know it?

"Do you remember any family members or siblings?" Asked the stranger.

There was a memory that flashed in his mind. No, he didn't want to remember. He shook his head. He didn't want to know anything else about Chase. He wanted Reginald back, why was he still Chase?

"Chase, what can you tell me about the broken door you always talk about?"

There was a clatter of metal on concrete. Broken. That's it, there was no escape now. It was time for Chase to admit his crimes. This man, he must be a pastor. This was confession. It made sense now. This was his Judgement Day.

"I broke the door." Hearing his own voice say it was like a splash of cold water. "I broke the washer. I broke the fence. I broke the car. I broke them. I broke everything. I broke the family." Rapidly, flashes of images, like a horror picture show, began to form. From fragments, a mirror began to come whole and the reflection was a demon named Chase.

He brought his fists to his head and tried to knock himself unconscious. He tore at his skin until there was only bone. Chase the demon who broke his home. A demon of rage and lust. A murderer. Wiggy... Wig... Wiggins. Troy Wiggins, son of the coffee maker. Chase remembered him. A voice pushed through the static. "Just close your eyes and forget I'm here."

Troy Wiggins. A well. They were walking along and wanted to make wishes. Troy wished for Maggie to fall in love him while Chase... Chase the demon, envious, angry, curious, sinful. It was an accident. It was no accident. Baptize, baptize, drowning, drowning, broken, broken...

That's why he was here, a place for demons. There was no escape anymore. Chase the boy was dead, Chase the demon was all that remained.

With time, the shadows lost their grip and began to slide back into the crevices from where they emerged. Even as the shadows faded, Maggie and Wiggie still didn't appear. He tried to force it, but he was too tired to speak. He was forced to lie alone as Chase, the young dead boy that broke everything. There was no escape or better place. When at last he heard the door close and he was alone, Chase hummed 'Eloise.' It made him feel better, as though he were remembering a tenderness that a mother should give. He closed his eyes, shoulders relaxed. As he thought, even the demons that appeared when his eyes were closed didn't emerge at all. He was completely alone.

Chase made himself smaller, hugging himself so tightly that it hurt, still humming the tune, clinging to it as though it was the only friend he had.

In the dead silence, as the darkness swallowed the yellow light, Chase heard a door squeal. Chase opened his eyes to trail to the beam of light coming through the door, blocked by a shadow. "…Troy?" There at the door was a young boy about twelve years old. His hair was as red as blood, green eyes reflecting the light. Chase stood from his bed. With quaking knees and trembling words, Chase stumbled forward. "I'm sorry."

Chase's body froze. Behind the child came the reaper, cloak red as guilt, gaze as ghostly as a graveyard. Chase looked back to Troy, but he was older now. "Broken," He whispered as red sap poured out of his mouth. His head cocked to an uncomfortable angle. The two figures began to twitch and close in on Chase.

There was a padded wall on his back. Chase tried to scream, but there was no sound. He tried to cry but there was no breath. He was drowning again. The liquid burned through his lungs and he was falling. Everything was getting darker. He saw the face of the reaper for a second and saw who it was. It was his mother. It was his brother. It was Wiggy. It was Maggie. It was his father. It was Reginald.

First, Chase could not see, then all he could feel was dizziness. He felt like he was falling, then he was floating. "Let's hope this works," He heard Reginald say before there was nothing left at all.

The very last thing that went through Chase's mind in the last second was denial. The very last desire Chase had was to run away as he always had. There was no need to remember what from.

There was no need to know where, or how, or why. He just needed to run.

ABOUT THE AUTHOR

The stories told in this book are inspired by the dreams and memories of the author. Jean has always loved to entertain and inspire people and hopes to continue to do so with the world they've created in which these stories take place. They tell these stories believing that everything can be a learning experience and that there is always a chance to learn something new.